THE UNEXPECTED SHELTER

APPLEBOTTOM MATCHMAKER SOCIETY

ABBY TYLER

SUMMARY

When the surprise son to Applebottom's mayor arrives in town and begins volunteering at the animal shelter, the town encourages the tender romance between him and the young woman who has run the shelter since her father's decline into dementia.

AbbyTyler
PO Box 160116
Austin, TX 78716
www.abbytyler.com

Paperback ISBN: 9781938150876

Edition 1.0

MEETING MINUTES

APPLEBOTTOM TOWN SQUARE PROPRIETORS
Gertrude Vogel, secretary
Because nobody else has a clue.

Today we met at the Applebottom Pie Shoppe, owned by yours truly.

Maude Lewis, co-owner of the pie shop, set out the nicest chess pie you ever did see for the others to take a gander at. Lemon chess with blueberries, pretty as you please.

I made it, of course.

As she sliced it, Mayor T-bone came in looking more serious than usual. Behind him was an interloper, a young man of maybe twenty-five.

T-bone stood in the doorway like a hanged man until Maude finally asked who the young man was.

Topher Smith-Cole, co-owner of Applebottom Blossoms, said the boy had to be kin. He was the spitting image of T-bone.

I figured he was right. They had the same eyes and nose, and the two of them had an uncanny way of standing in the same position.

"Well, spit it out," I said. "You already broke the sanctity of the Town Square Proprietors by bringing in a stranger."

"This ain't no stranger," T-bone said. "He's my son."

The room went wild with chairs scraping back and people gasping like T-bone done announced he was from Nebraska.

Topher and Danny recovered first, standing up to shake the boy's hand. Delilah sat there with her mouth open like she just swallowed a bug.

I finally said what everybody was thinking. "How in the world did you keep him a secret all this time?"

T-bone shrugged. "I didn't know. He showed up a couple days ago. We ran it by Micah and got all the legal paperwork square."

"Is he staying?" Betty asked.

"I reckon you can ask him yourself," T-bone said.

"Well, introduce him proper," Maude said.

"I'm Luke Southard," the boy said, shaking hands all around.

Everybody settled down and Maude finished cutting the pie. I noticed she gave Luke the first slice.

"Turns out a woman I knew back in the day had a

kid and didn't tell me," T-bone said. "Luke's a mechanic, and I figure we needed one of those around here."

"We surely do," Delilah said. "I had to haul my minivan all the way to Branson. Cost a hundred dollars just to tow!"

"Where will you set up shop?" Betty asked.

Luke swallowed his bite of pie. "T-bone has an outbuilding we're gonna empty out at the RV park."

Everybody went on and on about how good it would be to have someone fixing cars right in town again.

But I kept my eyeball on that boy. Sort of strange, turning up like this after twenty-five years. Good-lookin' too.

No doubt he'd be turning the local girls' heads.

Betty was thinking the same thing, as she caught my gaze across the table and gave me a quick nod.

We better work fast if we wanted to have a say in the matter of who got matched with the mayor's son.

Since nobody had anything for the agenda, we drank some coffee and talked about nothing special.

At least not in front of the boy.

Meeting adjourned.

CHAPTER 1

Savannah Perkins was pretty sure her life consisted of only two things – kibble and poop.

She hefted a giant bag of dog food on her shoulder and carefully stepped along the round paving stones that safely lead her from the food storage shed to the kennels.

The recent rains had turned the entire free-range yard for the dogs into a muddy pit. She had to stick to the path, because she couldn't tell for sure the difference between the kicked up bits of mud and the poop she'd be cleaning up later. The sky had sprinkled off and on that morning before she could get to yard patrol. Why couldn't dog poop be blue or something, easy to spot?

Sergeant, a tall German Shepherd with a patch of dark hair circling one eye, trotted toward her.

He was the current alpha at the animal shelter. The

rest of the dogs scurried after him, all approaching her as she made her way to the kennels for feeding time.

Savannah blew a stray hair out of her face and glanced up at the sky. The wind was changing. That meant a cold front was blowing in. She'd have to get the dogs in soon or end up with an entire pack of wet shivering pups that she'd have to towel down.

Where was her volunteer? She could have sworn one was coming today.

She shoved the new bag of kibble on a high shelf, well out of reach of any of the dogs, and took a second to catch her breath.

Sergeant stood for a moment near the open door and watched her. If she started filling the kibble bowls, he would lead the pack inside to settle in their kennels.

When Savannah moved toward the sick bay, Sergeant turned aside and trotted back out into the yard.

Actually, forget the human helpers. Sergeant was Savannah's greatest ally at the shelter. He taught the new arrivals the routine, alerted Savannah to any outliers in health or behavior, and generally kept the pack in line.

Currently, she had ten dogs, which was about all she could handle on her own. Seven of them were out in the yard with Sergeant. One, a terrified Chihuahua named Pixie, had still never been coaxed from his kennel even though they kept the door open.

Savannah would check on him in a moment.

First, though, she wanted to see to the puppies.

She leaned in to look inside the sick-bay kennel set up on the table in the back corner. A heat lamp kept the clear plastic dome at a consistent temperature. The bed was lined with soft blankets, and in the center, two four-week-old Rottweiler puppies curled together in a ball.

Savannah checked the clock over the kennel. It was time for their feeding.

She'd wake them in a minute. She ought to look in on the cat room.

She squeezed between two stacks of carriers, the ones she used when she had adoption days down at Delilah's doggy bakery. The screen door squeaked as she opened it.

This used to be a sunroom, something her dad had built when Savannah was a baby. Now it was a cat sanctuary. Ten kitties in various colors, breeds, and ages, lounged on cat trees by the wall of windows. Most of them were asleep, but a few of the youngest prowled the room, tossing catnip mice around or jumping each other.

The cat fountain was squealing, as it often did, and Savannah tapped it with her foot to make it go silent.

Sweetie, a white Persian with long fluffy hair peered up at her.

"You're the reason the filter's always clogged," Savannah said.

Sweetie paid her no mind, drinking in her preferred

way, her head under the flow of water, her little pink tongue lolling out to catch stray drops.

The litter boxes were full, another chore she would get to once she had shoveled out the yard while the dogs ate. Which would happen after she fed the puppies.

The days stretched out long, one the same as every other. The only things that ever seemed to change were the names and breeds and health conditions of animals in her care, and occasionally the faces of the volunteers.

When they showed.

She hurried back to the puppies, who were stirring and stretching. One of them had the tiniest little cast on his leg. Savannah had found them herself, her intuition leading her to the creek just off Table Rock Lake where puppies were regularly abandoned. It always seemed this time of year she'd find one or two or a whole litter down by the rocks.

She checked each time she went into town, and three days ago, there they were. She'd named them Tom and Jerry. They were mostly black with the usual markings, light brown cheeks and chests and paws. Tom had an injured leg. She suspected he'd been thrown in the river and hit a rock. She didn't understand people.

But he was healing up fine. In fact both the pups were thriving. They'd just had their first softened meal of solid food yesterday and could poop and pee on their own.

Another week in the private sick bay and she'd start introducing them to the smaller members of the pack.

Savannah pulled two bottles of formula from the fridge and heated them up in the little bottle heater she kept by the sick-bay kennel.

Both pups had already started to understand the routine, wobbling toward her as she pulled the bottles out and checked the temperature.

She lowered the side of the kennel and spread out the blanket, encouraging them to come closer. She sat on a stool and fed them both at the same time, glancing over her shoulder to make sure Sergeant still had the rest of the dogs under control in the yard.

She was only halfway through the bottles when the front doorbell rang. Great. Who was that?

"Boone!" she called. "Can you get the door?"

She heard a shuffling of feet, and she knew her dad was headed to the front of the house. Hopefully it was somebody they knew.

"Drink up, pups," she said. Tom finished first and staggered sleepily, milk drunk, back to the center of the blanket where it was warmest.

"Hurry up, Jerry," she said. The middle-of-the-night feedings were her cuddle time with them. Morning was get-it-down-and-go.

She heard a male voice, low and rumbling, definitely not her father's. She wondered what was going on out there. Worry gnawed at her belly. Her dad didn't always know what to do with people at the door.

Jerry got sleepy as the bottle grew to the end, so she

went ahead and cut him off and tucked him in next to his brother.

She pushed her hair off her forehead, grimacing as she felt the sticky wetness of warm milk smearing from her fingers. She wasn't going to win any beauty pageants today, that was for sure.

She was about to head to the front to see who the visitor was, praying it was a new volunteer and not a drop off that she couldn't take right now, when the sound of raindrops on the tin roof forced her to change direction.

Boone would have to handle the visitor. She needed to get the dogs in before they got drenched.

She hurried to the back door. "Sergeant," she called. "Bring everybody in."

Sergeant tried to lead the pack inside, but they were distracted by the storm. Luigi, a boxer-pug mix, was particularly prone to wallowing in the mud when he got the chance. As Sergeant attempted to herd the other dogs toward their kennels, Luigi plopped down in a shallow depression in the yard and rolled around on his back.

"Luigi," she called. "Come on."

A peal of thunder caused many of the dogs to jump and bark in fright. Savannah hurried out in the rain to shoo the dogs into the kennel room more quickly. Luigi was still on his back.

She squatted down to push him toward the back door. "Come on, Luigi. This is no time to play outside."

The rain picked up another notch, drenching her hair and shirt. "Come on, puppy dog. Let's go inside."

She would have to pick him up in a moment and see to the other dogs, even if would get her muddy. The pack was clearly distressed, only a few of them actually going to their kennels. Their muddy paws left trails everywhere on the concrete floor. She'd have to mop on top of everything else.

A tall figure appeared at the back door. Savannah peered through the rain, trying to make out who it was. Jesse? He hadn't volunteered for a couple months, but maybe he was back. She could definitely use his help and would ask no questions about his disappearance.

"Can you get the dogs squared away in there?" she called. "I'm trying to get Luigi in."

He nodded and turned back. Had to be Jesse.

She got down on her knees, grimacing as her jeans slid in the muck. It's just mud, she told herself. She suddenly recalled her mother's singsong voice. *God made dirt, so dirt can't hurt.*

She pushed on Luigi until she got him on his feet. With an unhappy grunt, Luigi finally yielded and started trotting toward the back door.

Savannah stood up. She was a fright, mud all over her hands and arms and knees and feet.

She used the rain to wash off the worst of it. Maybe Jesse could watch over the dogs for a moment while she went to change.

She shoved her hair off her face as she ducked inside

the kennel room, knowing she was streaking mud across her forehead. Couldn't be helped.

"How are they?" she asked, then stopped short. *Wait. Who was that?*

The man turned around, and Savannah took two steps back.

"Oh my gosh. Who are you?"

The man was disarmingly good-looking, with short dark hair that laid smoothly over to one side. He wore a T-shirt with a plaid button-down over it, the sleeves rolled up to the elbows.

"I'm Luke Southard," he said. "I don't believe we've met." He extended a hand.

Savannah lifted her arm, then realized it was covered with streaks of mud and withdrew it.

Strangers in Applebottom were rare. The town was off the beaten path. Most of the tourists stayed in nearby Branson. And certainly, people who were just passing through didn't stop by the animal shelter.

"I'm sorry. I've been wrestling Luigi in the yard. Why are you here?" She shoved her hair back, and realized she probably just put another streak of mud on her face.

"The lady who owns the dog bakery sent me. Said you could use some help."

Delilah, God bless her. But who was this man?

"I know everybody in Applebottom," she said. "But not you."

He moved suddenly to the side, blocking Luigi, who

was trying to escape out the back again. Savannah lunged for the door and shut it.

"Thanks."

"No problem." His grin made her belly flip over. "I'm new in town. It's a bit of a story, but it turns out T-bone is my pop."

"T-bone? The mayor?" Nobody would see this coming. But now that he said it, Savannah spotted the resemblance.

"That very one." He bent down to scratch Luigi behind the ears. The overweight lump flipped on his back immediately to get belly rubs instead.

"I'll be working on cars in the mornings, but I was in veterinary school up north before moving down. Delilah thought helping you out would look good as I tried to switch to a college down here."

Savannah felt absolutely faint. A new man in town. Son of a local. Ridiculously handsome.

And studying to be a veterinarian.

That was it.

She was dead.

CHAPTER 2

*L*uke Southard looked up at the prettiest girl he'd met in a long time while he scratched an overweight pug's belly.

She was streaked head to shoe with mud and soaking wet to boot. Some people might have said she looked like something the cat dragged in, but Luke could bear witness to the fact that it was actually a *dog* that caused her predicament. The one he was scratching.

"I figured I might have a few hours a day to come and help out," he said.

She stammered, and Luke couldn't tell if she was overwhelmed or just cold from the rain.

"Th-thank you. I mean, really. *Thank you.*"

Luke glanced around. A few of the pups had gone inside the kennels, like they knew where to be. The others, including this overweight fella at his feet, were loose among the rows.

"What would you have me do with them?" he asked. "You look like you might want a change of clothes and a hot drink."

"I could. I would. Please. I would love to change." Her hands fluttered all around as she pointed to one part of the room, then the other. "I already fed the babies. I just checked on the cats. I have to mop the floor. I won't be able to muck the yard until it stops raining."

He stood up. "Slow down. I can help. Do you want these fellas in their cages?"

"I think they're okay for the moment. I just need to feed them. I don't have the amounts written down anywhere, though, so it will have to wait on me. It's all up here." She tapped her wet head.

"How about you point me in the direction of some towels so I can dry some of these guys off."

"Yes. Perfect." She whirled around and opened a cabinet along the wall. "There's a bunch of old towels down here."

She headed for the side door he'd used when he came into the kennel room. The old man had shown him the way. He should ask her about that. The man had said some things that Luke hadn't quite understood, and he seemed confused. But that could wait. Right now, he needed to dry down some pups.

He pulled a towel off the stack, listening to her retreating footsteps. Then they quickly came back. He looked up from the pug, who was still on his back on the ground.

"Everything okay?"

Her face was flushed underneath the streaks of mud. "I think I forgot to introduce myself," she said. She held out her hand a second time, realized once again that it was muddy, and withdrew it. "I'm Savannah. These days, I run this animal shelter."

He grinned. "Nice to meet you, Savannah."

Her face flushed even more pink, and she hurried off again.

He bent down to clean off the pug's paws. What had she called him? Luigi? Like Donkey Kong?

"Is that your name?" he asked the dog. "Luigi?"

The pug let out a little yip.

Luke rolled him over to get the rest of him dry. He couldn't be all pug. He was too big, like a pug face on a boxer body. "That's not a very manly bark for a dog your size," he said. "I'm guessing you're a lover, not a fighter."

The dogs were pretty well behaved for a pack of mutts, he'd give her that. As he dried off each dog, he checked their tag to learn their names. The kennels had tiny whiteboards affixed to the top with the name of the dog who resided there.

A few resisted both the drying off and the move to a

kennel. One was a little dachshund named Ollie. Ollie followed Luke around as he checked all the kennels.

The other was Luigi, who seemed to think he was now owed a lifetime of belly rubs.

In the back corner of the kennel room, a German Shepherd sat upright on a large dog bed like he owned the place. He must be the house dog. Luke kneeled before him. His tag read Sergeant. Fitting.

"Nice to meet you, Sergeant," he said.

At his name, Sergeant's long nose lifted, and his warm black eyes met Luke's.

This was why he did it. Animals were more like humans than people gave them credit for. He could sense Sergeant sizing him up, probably deciding whether or not he was good enough to be around his pack. This was the alpha, no doubt about it. Luke had seen him herding everyone inside and keeping order while Savannah tried to deal with the pug.

"You and I are going to get along just fine," he assured Sergeant, holding out a fist for the dog to sniff.

The German Shepherd snubbed him and laid his head back down on his paws. All right. Sergeant would need to be convinced. He liked that.

"I don't trust most anybody either," he said. "So you and I are the same."

Sergeant kept an eye on Luke as he stood, taking the place in. There were two puppies under a heat lamp in an enclosed plastic bay. And she'd mentioned cats.

But a whole wall of kennels stood empty, suggesting the shelter used to hold more. He suspected Savannah was maxed out on what she could handle on her own. She needed more help. He was here to give it.

CHAPTER 3

*B*y the end of the day, Savannah was definitely ready to collapse. She usually felt this way, but today had been extra challenging with the arrival of the storm. The rain meant the dogs were cooped up more than usual. The thunder meant they were more skittish. And there had been extra chores, drying them off and cleaning up the mud. Plus more general interaction, so they wouldn't simply howl in their kennels all day.

Luke had proven very helpful. He played with the dogs in the narrow aisles between the cages. He'd fed the puppies their afternoon meal. And when the rain stopped, he'd even volunteered to muck out the yard, which couldn't have been easy with all the mud.

Savannah fed him lunch, just sandwiches and chips, and he had promised to come back the next day.

She sat in the living room recliner with her feet up,

an arm crossed over her face. Even though she'd had help today, Luke's presence had added a more formal element, and she hadn't been able to relax. Maybe as she got to know him, things would get easier.

The shuffle of Boone's feet on the hardwood floor made her shift her arm and turn toward the doorway.

Her father entered the room like a man twenty years older than he was. Savannah's eyes pricked as she watched him slowly navigate the sofa to sit in her mother's old rocking chair.

"Would you like your recliner?" she asked.

He held up a hand, although Savannah wasn't quite sure what he meant by it. It could mean no. Or he could be asking her not to speak because it confused him. Or he might just be trying to hide the fact that something else was going on inside his head.

Boone rocked back and forth, humming a little song under his breath. He looked like a farmer in overalls and a long-sleeved flannel shirt. He hadn't always dressed this way. Those were his father's clothes. Boone had found a trunk full of them a couple years back and adopted his father's manners.

He'd grown up on a farm proper, and something in the mixed-up regions of his mind these last few years led him to believe that he ought to dress like one now. Among Savannah's problems, this wasn't one that concerned her.

"I'm going to make some spaghetti for dinner," she said. "You like that."

Boone didn't respond, almost as if he hadn't heard her. His eyes were closed, his long gray eyelashes lying against his ruddy cheeks. He was still well-built and strong, and his capable hands held onto the round end of the rocker arm. But the dementia had its grip on him. There was no going back to the old Boone.

Her father had opened this animal shelter twenty years ago, shortly after Savannah's mother died. Lena had loved taking in strays, and there had always been a half-dozen dogs and cats around. After the accident, Boone gave up his job as the head custodian at the elementary. With the little bit of money they got from the drunk driver's insurance company, and a charter with the City of Applebottom, he'd opened the shelter in her name. He needed to stay home with his small daughter, and opening Lena's Home for Strays helped him honor his wife. It was the only life Savannah had ever known.

She sat a few minutes more, watching her father rock in her mother's chair, then got up to put the spaghetti on to boil. It was a simple life, and she didn't resent it.

But the arrival of this new man certainly changed things. Savannah glanced around the shabby kitchen, the linoleum on the floor curling up at the edges. The counters had worn spots, and a few burns here and there from when she was learning to cook and didn't realize a hot pan couldn't go directly onto a Formica countertop.

But it was home. She'd been three years old when her mother was lost to her, so there were only impressions that remained, ghostly memories faded by time.

But at odd moments, particularly when Savannah was melancholy as she was now, she sensed her mother's presence. Sometimes it was the scent of lemon soap that brought her back, the image of Mama standing near the sugar jar, drying her hands. Or in the sunroom, a fleeting glimpse of her sitting at the wicker table in the corner while Savannah played on the floor.

Savannah didn't question this. Her mother was a part of this house, and a part of her. Sometimes when Boone was particularly poorly, Savannah would enter his room to bring him his morning coffee, and he would call her Lena. She knew she favored her mother. She'd seen the pictures. It was just nature's way of keeping her mother close.

Her father's diagnosis had come about the time Savannah thought she might take off on an adventure of her own. After graduating high school, she worked hard to find a steady flow of volunteers to help her father, which would enable her to leave. Fisher College had added the shelter to their list where veterinary and vet tech candidates could get their work hours completed.

But then little things started to happen. Boon would forget to feed the cats. He'd call the animals by the wrong names.

The volunteers all laughed it off, because who could keep track of all these ever-changing fur babies coming in and out of their lives? They often had forty or fifty at a time.

But Savannah had known. Her father had always taken each of their rescues into his heart.

The money problems came next. Forgotten bills. Un-ordered supplies. A snafu with the volunteers where they didn't get credit for the work they had done, causing a bit of an uproar at the college. Savannah had tried to smooth all that out, but it was never completely fixed and their shelter got a reputation for not being well run.

The worst day had been when Boone had confused a pretty young volunteer with his dead wife. He came up from behind and wrapped his arms around her, setting off a harassment investigation that severed their relationship with the volunteer program.

Savannah had no choice but to stay, taking Boone to the doctors, relieved that there was a diagnosis to hang his behavior on. She didn't blame the college for cutting them off. The only volunteers that came after that were families from Applebottom, those who could vouch for Boone and understood what was happening. Savannah reduced the number of animals she would accept, creating a foster network for the others.

She hung onto the minimum required to keep the charter with the town. Without their money, they'd certainly be sunk.

She kept hanging on. On some days, Boone was still Boone. He'd walk into the kitchen and ask about the feed orders, the repairs that needed to be made to the kennels of the fence. His mind would clear.

Then just as quickly he was gone again, his shuffle back, the droop of his shoulders. He seemed to accept her always, for which she was grateful. She could manage.

And now she had help.

CHAPTER 4

$\mathcal{L}$uke sat on a chair on the porch of the convenience store at T-bone's RV Park, a cold can of RC Cola in his hand. T-bone sat next to him, his legs kicked out, his heavy biker boots crossed at the ankle. Luke hadn't been able to think of T-bone as his father yet. It was all pretty new.

Truth be told, he'd considered heading back to Montana. But the old ladies at the pie shop had convinced him to go check out Fisher College, and he found that their program was just as reputable and good deal cheaper. With T-bone offering him an abandoned camper that he could fix up, his expenses would be virtually nothing. Plus he had a steady stream of mechanic work, and something about the people here had made him feel right at home.

So he'd stayed.

The RV Park was quiet. Early fall was always a dead

time, T-bone told him. The few people renting spots were driven inside by the storms from earlier.

Even so, most evenings meant people hanging out on the artificial beach T-bone had constructed on the shore of the lake. They burned fires in the pits and played music.

But not tonight. The temperature had fallen considerably, making hanging out by the water less hospitable. Luke generally liked the noise and the people. But right now, the silence felt right.

T-bone's voice rumbled in the half dark. "So what did you think of that girl?"

Luke knew who he meant. Savannah. She'd cleaned up right nice while he managed the dogs. He liked how natural she was. The long brown hair, faded jeans, and sweatshirt. "Seems she's got a lot on her plate."

T-bone let out a little snort in agreement.

"What's with the old man who lives there? He didn't seem well." Savannah hadn't even brought him up, and Luke didn't think he ought to ask on his first day.

"Dementia," T-bone said.

"Is that her dad? She called him Boone."

"Yeah. Everybody calls him Boone."

"She got a mom?"

"Drunk driver killed her when Savannah was three."

"Oh. Dang."

T-bone stretched his arms out and clasped his hands behind his head. The chains fastened to his belt jangled as he shifted on the chair. "Boone took the money and opened that shelter. It's named after her mom."

"Heckuva thing."

They fell silent, looking out over the park. Luke had a lot of questions for his father, but he didn't know how to ask. Why hadn't he ever found a wife? Had he ever thought about Luke's mother? Did he plan to stay in Applebottom forever?

But Luke knew the most important things. That T-bone was an honest man. That the community here trusted him. That he owned the RV Park free and clear and was happy to pass it on to Luke if Luke wanted it when the time came. That was too far ahead for Luke to think about.

T-bone hadn't known Luke's mother was pregnant, and she'd taken off with some other man anyhow. Even though T-bone seemed stuck in his bachelor ways, Luke felt certain he'd have done his part if he'd known. Only when his mother was near-death from cancer had she given him all the letters to T-bone she'd never sent. That was how Luke had found him.

"You think she's going to be able to keep that shelter open, what with her dad and all?" Luke asked.

"She's managed so far."

The clouds shifted, revealing the full moon over the lake. The water was choppy, the wind still high from the storm. The air smelled clean and cool. Luke hadn't arrived in time to get back into vet school for the fall, so he had a semester to kill. He hoped the work he was doing at the shelter would help his chances of moving his credits. He was waiting to hear from the advisor about how the transfer might work.

He finished his cola and tossed the can toward the recycle bin in the corner of the porch. "Gonna hit the hay," he told T-bone.

"You going back there tomorrow?"

"Yeah. There's a section of fence that the little dogs can squeeze through. Gonna patch that up."

T-bone nodded. "I'm proud of you, son. You do right by that little girl."

Savannah was no little girl. But Luke knew what he meant. He'd only been in Applebottom a few weeks. Nobody knew if Luke was a saint or a scoundrel, not even T-bone. And given his lifestyle up till now, the latter was probably a better assessment.

But Savannah was different. He'd met a lot of people with lives as tough as his had been. Most of them had given in to a bleak existence. Luke wasn't that much better, his vet classes being his only real effort toward an honest living. But Savannah had held onto something most people in bad circumstances gave up on. Optimism. She hadn't let life beat her down.

She was exactly the sort of person he ought to be around.

CHAPTER 5

The next morning, Savannah pointed at herself in the mirror and said, "You are trying too hard."

Boone walked past the open door and paused for a moment. "If you keep talking to yourself, people will think you're crazy."

Then he shuffled on.

Savannah doubled over with giggles. Trust Boone to make a smart-aleck response. He must be having a good day. At least as good as they get lately.

She stepped out into the hallway to watch his retreating figure. Yes, there was less shuffle in his step. This day was already turning out to be a good one.

And soon there would be Luke.

She turned back to the mirror. "I have my eye on you," she said to herself. She'd spent the morning alternating styles between ponytails, braids, hair down, hair half-down. She had to appear like she was just working, but she had to look good, too.

It was maddening.

In the end, she settled on a French braid, a tiny bit of mascara, and Chapstick with just a touch of color.

Probably anything other than covered in mud would be an improvement over yesterday anyway.

When she made it into the kitchen, Boone was sitting at the wobbly breakfast table, holding a butter knife and a fork.

"You making flapjacks today?" he asked.

Savannah's heart fell a little. Asking for flapjacks meant that Boone wasn't quite in the here and now after all. Boone's mother, now long dead, called pancakes flapjacks, but Savannah's mother never had.

She simply answered, "Absolutely." She didn't have time to make any from scratch this morning, but she kept extra pancakes in the freezer so she could quickly heat up a few. She had most things ready to defrost in case Boone asked for them. Sometimes he got agitated if he didn't get what he asked for. She'd learned the hard way to be prepared.

Within a couple minutes, she had a plate of steaming pancakes topped with butter and syrup ready for him to eat.

"Would you like me to cut those up for you?" she asked.

"Oh no," he said. "I can do it."

He began sawing through the stack. It wasn't going

well, but probably he would manage to eat it on his own. Savannah had to walk a fine line here. If he got frustrated, he could blow up in anger. But if she helped him when he didn't want it, he'd blow up anyway.

Savannah glanced at the clock. Luke had said he would come by around eight. He didn't have any car work this morning, so he planned to put in a full day at the shelter.

Savannah wanted to send up a little *hallelujah* that a couple bigger projects were going to get attended to today. Some holes in the fence. Rotating the sacks of kibble to make sure she was using the oldest bags first. The last several deliveries had just been tossed in there willy-nilly, and she knew she needed to get to the ones closer to the bottom.

Yes, this was going to be a better day for sure.

When she opened the door to the kennel room, a chorus of barks drowned out everything. She was a little behind schedule due to her extra primping, and the dogs definitely wanted to be let out.

She bent down, releasing all the latches, and hurried to the back door to spring it open.

Sergeant strolled out from his bed and followed the pack outside. Savannah knew she could count on him to keep them fairly corralled until she could feed the cats, come back around to the puppies, and haul in that day's bag of kibble.

She felt supercharged, despite her middle-of-the-night feeding with the wee ones. She wouldn't have to do that much longer. Tom and Jerry were growing fit and strong. Maybe tonight she'd slide their latest feeding to bedtime and stretch them all the way to the next morning. Since they were experimenting with their first solids, it was probably time.

She also ought to call Dr. Black out to check on Tom's leg. At least the puppy was her only current health crisis, although she still worried about the Chihuahua who wouldn't leave his kennel. Maybe she would have time today to work with him a little bit on that.

She hauled down a bag of cat food and filled the bowls along the wall of the sunroom. That accomplished, she headed to the kennels, peeking out at the dogs, who all seemed to be behaving, and grabbed two bottles of formula from the fridge. She propped her phone on the side of the sick-bay kennel, glancing through a list of her emails as the puppies drank greedily.

They were mostly the usual things. Delivery reminders. A bazillion sales solicitations as if she could afford fancy new dog beds or the highest rated organic dog food. Just the formula for Tom and Jerry was killing her budget. Thank goodness they'd be totally switched to solids in the next week or two.

She spotted an email from Delilah about adoption day, and set down a bottle for a second to open it.

Apparently, Delilah had been getting quite a few inquiries about pets. Delilah knew that Savannah had been overwhelmed lately and figured that an adoption day would be easier to manage than sending a bunch of random people out to the shelter.

Savannah sighed. The hard part about adoption day was for her to be gone from the house. She had to time it just right, when the animals she left behind were mostly settled and could manage without supervision. And there was always Boone. There were days when she didn't feel like she should leave him either, but he didn't do so well if she brought him down to the Square. He had a tendency to wander, and he didn't always discern the difference between walking on the sidewalk and down the middle of Main Street.

The day Delilah was proposing was a Saturday, of course, the day most people would be going through her shop. But Savannah didn't know if she would have Luke's help. Maybe she could call out Gayle. She sometimes volunteered on weekends even though Savannah hadn't seen her much over the summer.

Tom finished his bottle but wasn't the least bit sleepy. She stroked his fuzzy little head, straightening one of his short little ears. She hated that Rottweilers had such a bad reputation. These were so cute.

When Jerry finished his bottle, Savannah picked up both of the pups and carried them outside, one in each hand. The pack was roaming the yard under the watchful eye of Sergeant. At first she tried to set the pups down near the door, but immediately, several of the dogs ran over to sniff out the babies.

Savannah picked them back up. She bumped her hip against the latch that separated the main yard from a smaller enclosed section where she kept aggressive dogs when they came her way.

She passed through and bumped it closed, and the other dogs lined up along the chain-link fence to get their eyes on the puppies.

Savannah set them down. The ground was still soft from the rains, but this area, which saw a lot less use, had tufts of grass.

The moment she set down Jerry, he toddled over to one of the patches of green and lifted his leg to pee.

"Good boy," Savannah said.

Tom was a lot less certain. His little cast was heavy and dragged along behind him as he tried to navigate the ruts in the dirt.

Eventually he managed to make his way to the same bit of grass, sniffing it where his littermate had relieved himself. He angled his body as if he would lift the casted leg, then realized that wasn't going to work and tried to lift the opposite one. But that put pressure on the hurt leg. He gave a little yelp.

"Poor pup," Savannah said. She stroked his head and lifted the little cast herself. A tiny stream of pee hit the grass.

"Get it all out, mind you," she said. "We're not going to be doing this for every nook and cranny of the yard."

The pack ran to the other corner of the fence, a

chorus of barks and yapping alerting her that someone was approaching.

She stood up and smoothed her shirt down, tucking the back into her waistband. It had to be Luke. She told him yesterday not to ring the bell in front, but come on around back. This would bypass Boone.

She was right. Luke reached over the chain-link fence to unlatch the gate. When he stepped inside, the dogs all jumped over each other to greet him.

He knelt down, giving each one a bit of attention.

That was enough for most of them, who were willing to resume wandering the yard. But Luigi immediately flopped down on his back for more of the belly rubs he got yesterday.

"He's spoiled now," Savannah called out.

"I reckon he probably could use a bit of spoiling," Luke said.

Savannah could not smile any bigger. What was it about this man that made her heart beat so fast?

He patted Luigi on the belly and stood up. As he headed toward her section of the yard, Luigi trotted along behind him. Luke had made a friend for life in that one.

Luke leaned against the fence that divided the yards. "You got the pups out."

"Tom here is trying to figure out how to lift his cast to pee."

"How long is that gonna be on there?"

"Doc Black said probably another week."

"He must've been pretty hurt."

Savannah nodded. "He couldn't use it at all when I first got him."

Luke glanced around the yard. "You need me to do something inside, or should I get to that fence straightaway?"

"You can haul in a bag of kibble from the food shed," she said. "I need to rotate the stock in there. The newest is currently on top."

"How about I go ahead and rearrange it. Then I'll hit the fence."

"Sounds good."

He hesitated. "I was thinking, if you wanted to add the amount of food you give each dog to those little whiteboards on their kennels, I could probably feed them. Since the amounts are currently only in your head." He gave her little wink.

That was actually a really smart idea. "I'll write it down today when I feed them."

He walked along the pavers to the shed, and Savannah had to force her gaze back to the puppies at her feet. Tom was already trying to wiggle beneath the gap to get into the main yard with the big dogs.

She rushed over and picked him up. "You're getting ahead of yourself," she said. "Those dogs would trample you in a New York minute."

She turned and lifted Jerry as well. "Let's get you guys back inside."

Savannah had emptied out the rest of yesterday's bag

of kibble and fed about half the dogs when Luke made it back inside with the fresh bag.

"Did you have enough to finish the feeding?"

"Not quite. But I wrote down everyone whose food bowl is already filled."

Luke set the bag on the floor. "Why don't you finish writing them out, and I'll fill the bowls. What's on your agenda today?"

"The cats are next. I need to clear the litter boxes and check on Tuxedo, who got spayed last week."

"I didn't notice any cones of shame when I peeked in yesterday." Luke leaned against the line of cages, and Savannah had to drag her eyes away from his strong forearms beneath the rolled up plaid sleeves.

"He only needed it for a couple of days. He's a healthy cat, and healed up quickly."

"All righty then."

Savannah kneeled with her dry erase marker and quickly wrote out the amounts of feed she gave each dog on their whiteboards. She felt Luke's eyes on her, and she warmed all over. It had been quite a while since she met somebody new.

She hadn't really dated anybody since Billy Ray, and that was right around when Boone got diagnosed. Since then, her life had become increasingly focused. Doctor visits, hard conversations, and putting out all the little fires that came with trying to run an animal shelter on your own.

Not that Boone was totally useless. He often sat in

the sunroom and played with the cats. He could also be counted on to watch over the tiny puppies. As long as he didn't do any of the riskier chores, like cooking on the stove or handling power tools, he could manage some of the quieter, easier tasks that they faced daily. When he wasn't grumpy, anyway.

She stood up, all the feed amounts documented on the boards. Luke moved along the kennels, filling bowls the prescribed amount.

"If you can refresh their water, that will be a help," she said.

"Will do."

She checked on the puppies. Tom had sacked out, his little cast buried in blankets. But Jerry hopped around, begging for attention.

Savannah opened the sick bay door and pulled him out. This was a good job for Boone.

"I'll be right back," she told Luke, and headed into the main house with the puppy.

Boone still sat at the kitchen table. He'd managed to eat a good portion of pancakes, but quite a bit was also on the table, with more falling to the floor.

She walked to the sink and wet a dish towel. "Hey Boone, can you take care of this puppy for a bit? He needs some attention."

The chair scraped back as Boone stood. She held Jerry in one hand while she wiped off the sticky syrup from Boone's hands with the other. When he was clean enough, she led him back to the living room and the big armchair. "Now don't let him on the ground. We don't want to lose him."

She settled Boone in the chair and put the footrest up to discourage him from taking off. She laid the blanket on his lap and set the puppy in the middle. Boone's large wrinkled hands closed around the puppy, fondling his little triangle ears. "Rottweiler," Boone said.

"That's right, Boone. His name is Jerry."

Her eyes sparked a little as Boone lifted the pup to his face and planted a gentle kiss on his head. Her father had always had a tender soul.

When she was sure they were settled, she headed back out to the kennel room. Luke had just emptied out the bag and was folding it up.

"There's a whole set of trash cans at the side of the house," she said. "We haul it into town every Tuesday."

Luke nodded. "I assume the tools in the shed that I spotted are what I should use on the fence."

"Sure. There's more in the garage though. You can cut through the house if the side door is locked." It probably was. She was more careful now. Not that she thought someone would get in. But she wanted to make sure Boone didn't get out.

"I'll go get started." He gave her a quick smile and headed out the back door.

Morning sure had gone smoothly with Luke's help.

She could get used to this.

📷

Luke whistled to himself as he knocked out a rotten section of board and replaced it with a fresh piece he'd scavenged from behind the shed.

He enjoyed tasks like this, simple and satisfying. Savannah kept the dogs in a smaller part of the yard while he worked. He caught glimpses of her as she went about her own chores, mucking the yard and adding to the compost in the field beyond the fence.

He guessed the shelter probably used to hold three times the number they currently had. He wondered where those animals went now, and if he could do something to help make sure they weren't being sent to any kill shelters in the area.

But looking at how Savannah handled herself with the pack, cooing and clucking and calling each dog by name, he figured she wasn't going to let that happen to any of the animals in her care. He admired how she managed to keep things running even when life seemed to be throwing one curveball after another her way. She had a good deal a fortitude.

The sun made quick work of drying out the ground from yesterday's rains. He patched up the most critical parts of the fence and put away the tools. As he came out of the shed, Savannah squinted up at the sky and said, "Looks to be high noon. You want to come in for lunch?"

He wondered if she fed all her volunteers. He'd tossed a couple granola bars from T-bone's convenience store in the passenger seat of his truck, but he figured after the way she made him sandwiches yesterday, she might be willing to do it again.

"You got yourself a date," he said and smiled a little inside when her cheeks turned pink. He definitely liked the girl. He liked her a lot.

When Luke made his way into the kitchen, Boone was sitting at the table. Luke was glad T-bone had let him know about the situation, so he was better prepared than he had been when he arrived yesterday to a confused man who let him inside the house without question.

In fact, he ought to talk to Savannah about that. If her dad was going to let just anybody in the door, she might want to think about how much freedom he had to open it.

Or maybe she already knew all that. He'd only known her twenty-four hours. He probably shouldn't interfere.

He sat down in the chair. "Good afternoon, sir," he said.

Boone paid him no mind.

Savannah stood at the counter, adding ham and cheese to hoagie rolls.

"I feel like I should bring lunch for you guys one of the days," Luke said.

"Nonsense," Savannah said. "It's the least we can do for all the time you're volunteering. You've been a huge help."

"You get a fair amount of volunteers?" Luke asked.

Savannah set plates down in front of him and Boone. "Lately we've been a little short."

Boone picked up a sandwich and took a bite. He looked at both of them with big innocent eyes as he chewed.

"I couldn't help but notice you have a lot of empty cages. Are there not a lot of animals, or do you find other places for the ones that come around?"

Savannah sat down with her plate. "I've been able to find foster homes for a lot of them. It's better that way anyhow. They get more love and care. I currently have about all I can handle when I'm working by myself."

That's what Luke had figured.

"It's a remarkably well-behaved pack," he said.

Savannah nodded. "My German Shepherd Sergeant is really good with them. Every once in a while a dog will try and challenge him, but for the most part, he manages the dogs as long as he's not too outnumbered."

"It's always great when you have a dog like that around."

They ate in silence for a few minutes, and Luke glanced around their kitchen. It was more or less tidy, a few dishes stacked in the sink. He wondered how she managed it all.

"What's the plan for the afternoon?" he asked.

"Delilah wants to have an adoption day this week-end," Savannah said. "That means I need to make sure I have enough carriers to transport them, and dig out the portable fencing to set up outside her shop. And I'll need to decide who gets to go."

"Is that a hard decision?"

She sat back in her chair. Wisps of hair framed her face. "Always. Do I take the cute ones and pretty much guarantee they'll get adopted? Do I take the ones that have been here the longest?"

"I think Luigi would win over the hearts of a lot of people," he said.

Boone spoke up unexpectedly. "You should take Lady out for a walk."

Savannah patted his hand. "I'll be sure to do that."

"Which one is Lady?" Luke asked.

Savannah smile turned a touch sad. "Oh, Lady was a bird dog we had when I was about five years old."

She collected the plates at the table and walked to the sink.

Luke stood and gathered his and Savannah's cups. Boone grabbed his suddenly and held it close to his chest. "Mine."

"Yes, sir," he said.

Savannah watched him from the sink. "We can talk about him later," she said. "He was diagnosed two years ago."

"T-bone gave me the short version," he said. "I'm just here to help."

She turned to stare out the kitchen window. "You don't know how grateful I am for that."

He was pretty sure he did.

CHAPTER 6

Saturday morning dawned bright and clear. Delilah had assured Savannah that there were at least three families serious about taking a dog. Savannah just had to decide which ones.

She wouldn't be taking any cats. Mrs. Fresno had fostered the latest kittens that had been brought to the shelter. They were at the stage where it was easiest to adopt them out, so Savannah was letting her handle that.

She would take four or five dogs.

Savannah headed into the kennel room. Franny had come to help her. Before she could even ask Luke about his availability, he had let her know that several members of Applebottom were bringing their cars to him Saturday morning. Gayle hadn't been available either, but Franny was willing.

When Savannah entered the kennel room, Franny

was sitting cross-legged on the floor in jeans and a flowered blouse. Her hair was a riot of light brown and gray curls. She looked up at Savannah in utter despair.

"They're all so sweet," she said. "I can't decide who we can part with, even if they will have a good home."

Savannah kneeled down next to her. " I was thinking of taking Pixie, the shy Chihuahua. Delilah said that one of the families had a very quiet little girl, and I think she might fall in love with him."

Fanny nodded. "You're so good at this. I don't see how you do it."

"Boone always said to fill 'em up with love and send them with your heart."

"He's such a good man. What about Luigi?"

Savannah pictured the pug with Luke and wondered if she could let him go. "I'm really trying to get his weight down before I send him away. I'm worried about his heart."

"All right. Ollie there is mighty cute." Fanny reached over and slid a ten-year-old chocolate brown dachshund into her lap. "He's not too big."

Savannah nodded, petting the dog's head. "You think you have time to give him a quick bath before we go?"

"Sure," Fanny said. She stood up and carried Ollie to the deep sink by the windows.

Not all the dogs were inside. Through the open back door, Savannah watched Sergeant stand guard over the larger dogs. They had a Labrador mix. Two pit bulls, one of which was super sweet. And a full-sized poodle who really needed grooming. Savannah wished she'd gotten to that last week.

Two of the three families had children. The Labrador would be great for either of those, if the one with the little girl didn't go for the Chihuahua.

The puppies were definitely too small, even though they'd probably be adopted immediately. She wasn't quite ready to let Tom and Jerry go.

So it was settled. The Chihuahua. A Labrador. A pit bull. The dachshund.

Could she take one more? She ought to.

Maybe Luigi *should* get his chance.

All right. She would take the pug. She reached down to scratch his belly. "Hopefully you'll stay close. Maybe we'll see you around town."

She would send special food with Luigi if he got adopted. She'd let the family know to help him slim down.

That settled, she headed over to the sick bay to feed Tom and Jerry their midmorning breakfast. Delilah's would open in about an hour, and they would show up about an hour after that. Flo had promised to come check on Boone during her lunch hour and sit with him. That meant he wouldn't be alone much at all. It would be all right.

While Franny bathed Ollie, Savannah brushed cornstarch through a few of their coats to clean them up a bit and gave each of them a minty dog bone to make sure they were sweet-smelling pups for their big day.

"I guess we better load them up," Franny said.

Most of the dogs went into their crates fairly easily, especially when bribed with bacon treats.

But Pixie, the Chihuahua, refused to come out of her kennel, cowering in the back.

Savannah lay on her belly on the floor.

"Oh, Pixie, I don't want to have to drag you out. This could be a good day for you. You might never have to go in a kennel again."

Franny came up beside her. "The others are already loaded. What are you going to do with this one?"

"I guess if I can't get her, I can take one of the others. Or we can just go with four."

"I'll go fetch the peanut butter from the kitchen," Franny said.

Good call. It was the treat of last resort.

Savannah lay there, the chorus of shuffles and the occasional bark from the other dogs filling the space as she looked at Pixie.

She was so little, clearly undernourished as a pup. Probably her skittishness came from a lack of nutrients early on. She saw this a lot.

Pixie had been found huddled in a shallow hole outside of an abandoned house in the woods. A couple of kids had come across her and tried to take her home, but their mother would have nothing of it. So the pup had come here.

Pixie never barked, never whined, and never wanted to come out of hir kennel. She did not follow the usual dog habit of never relieving themselves where they slept, and for this reason, Savannah kept towels at the bottom of her cage instead of a bed. Twice a day, she went in and replaced the soiled one with a new one.

Doc Black said she was fine and healthy, just skittish. She could be house trained, surely, if she had quiet and patience from someone.

It would take a special family to want her. If she didn't go today, Savannah would try to work with her more. With Luke's help, she might be able to make some progress.

Franny returned with a glob of peanut butter on the end of a dog bone.

The smell of it perked Pixie up considerably. Her tiny ears lifted.

"That's good," Savannah said. "I think it might be her kryptonite."

The two of them backed away from the kennel and set the peanut butter bone on the ground.

Savannah moved aside and lifted a towel from the top of the cages. She really hoped they could get her. She had a feeling this little girl was just the right ticket.

Pixie's quivering nose emerged from the edge of the kennel. Savannah and Franny glanced up at each other, their eyes wide.

Come on, Pixie.

Her tiny head lifted, looking first at Savannah, then over at Franny. They didn't dare move.

One tremulous paw rested on the cement floor. Then the other.

Savannah could barely breathe.

She took a few more steps, and her little pink tongue flicked out to lick the peanut butter.

Savannah moved in inches. She could not startle the pup now.

Slowly she lowered the blanket until it blocked the way back to Pixie's kennel.

Pixie continued to lick the peanut butter, oblivious to the movement behind her.

Savannah carefully draped the towel over her. Pixie startled and crouched low to the ground. But she didn't bolt.

"Good baby," Savannah said. "Come here."

She picked up Pixie, then the bone, and made sure she got to continue to eat the treat.

The tiny dog quivered in her arms, but she didn't scramble or try to get away. This was a good sign.

"This is great," Franny said. "I think if one of us just holds her the whole time, everyone will want to take a look.

"I'm going to be picky about who might want her though," Savannah said. "She can't just go anywhere."

"True. That quiet little girl might have a big noisy sibling."

Savannah passed the dog to Franny, and they headed through the house.

Boone sat in his armchair, watching television.

Savannah kissed his head. "Your sister Flo is going to be here in less than half an hour," she said.

"Transportation for one hundred," Boone said.

Savannah glanced at the screen. It was "Wheel of Fortune," not "Jeopardy." She patted his shoulder.

When Franny and Pixie were settled in the passenger seat, and the truck rumbled down the dirt lane to the road, Franny said, "So I hear the mayor's son has been helping you."

"Just the last two days. He had to fix cars this morning."

"Has he been useful?"

"Definitely. He mended the fences and organized the food shed. We have a new system for feeding the dogs. I'm telling you, just one other person full time, and I can run this like clockwork."

"Too bad there's no money to hire anyone." Franny held the dog bone so that Pixie could keep licking the peanut butter. "I heard the boy was easy on the eyes."

Savannah didn't answer that. The old truck bumped onto the highway.

But Franny didn't let it go. "Have you thought about who you're going to take to Anna's wedding?"

"Haven't given it a thought," Savannah said. "I didn't think I needed to take anybody."

"You know Billy Ray's going, right?"

"What?" Billy Ray hadn't been around Applebottom in over a year. "I thought he took a job down in Pine Bluff."

"Got fired," Franny said. "His mama told me."

"Doesn't surprise me," Savannah said.

"He was asking about you. Asked if you were still running the shelter. Like maybe you needed help."

That was all she needed, Billy Ray sniffing around, trying to see if he could cash in on the fact that she had a house and a living.

"I'm not interested in seeing him," she said. "He did me wrong, and I have no use for a man like that."

"I see," Franny said. "I just wanted to give you a warning."

"Thank you. I don't get much gossip at the shelter these days."

All the rest of the way into Applebottom, Savannah stewed over what Franny said. What was Anna thinking, asking Billy Ray to her wedding? Hadn't Savannah made clear they were over? Was Anna thinking of putting them back together?

Savannah hadn't told anybody what had happened. It was humiliating, learning your man had taken up with another girl on the side. She wasn't local, so maybe nobody knew.

Now he would be at the wedding. And seeking her out.

Savannah was one of the bridesmaids. She couldn't exactly get out of going.

The old truck lumbered into Applebottom, and Savannah turned toward Town Square. She needed to put Billy Ray from her mind. She had two weeks until the wedding to figure something out, and these doggies needed her full attention.

The old Volvo was a solid car, but it was getting on in years.

Luke trained his ear to listen to the engine as he rolled down the highway between T-bone's RV Park and the town.

There was a gremlin in the engine, and Luke would find it. This was his third car to work on today, and he had hoped to return it to its owner tonight. But not if the problem didn't present itself.

He turned down one of the side streets, passing some of the older houses of Applebottom.

He didn't mean to drive into Town Square proper, but he didn't know his way around perfectly yet. He realized too late that the tiny side street he had taken dumped him directly into the Square.

No harm done. He would just pass through and head off the other direction.

He had just paused to wait for a car to pull out from in front of the dog bakery, when he spotted Savannah.

She sat outside on the sidewalk between two pens. A chalkboard sign read *Adoption Day*.

Which dogs did she have with her?

When the other car was clear, Luke slid into the spot.

Right as he killed the engine, he heard it. The chugging, the missing on one cylinder. It might just be clogged.

But nevermind that. He'd handle it when he got back to his shop. He wanted to see how the adoptions were going.

When he stepped out of the car, a curly-haired woman sitting on a folding chair next to Savannah looked up and saw him. She nudged Savannah.

Savannah glanced around, then spotted him herself. "Hey, Luke." She patted the dog in her lap. It was the shy Chihuahua who wouldn't leave his kennel.

"You got her out," Luke said.

"Franny did," Savannah said, turning to the woman. "Franny, have you met Luke?"

Franny stood up and extended a hand. "Only from the rumors. Nice to meet you."

"Nothing too terrible I hope," Luke said.

"Not so far, but with T-bone as your father, one never can tell." Franny grinned at him, so he knew she was just teasing him. That was one thing he hadn't quite gotten used to yet in Applebottom. Everyone talked so familiarly, like they had known you forever.

Luke turned to Savannah. "Have you had to let any of them go?"

"Ollie got snapped up right away," Savannah said.

"The dachshund?"

She nodded. "I have one family who is seriously considering Winston."

"That's the pit bull, right?"

"Yes. I'm so excited for that."

"No takers for your shy one?"

"We're hoping a family with a little girl is going to come look at him. We think he might be a good fit."

Luke bent down in front of the Chihuahua, mainly as an excuse to keep his eyes on Savannah. She was such a down-to-earth girl in her jeans and Applebottom high school sweatshirt.

He heard a little whine from the pen and peered past Franny.

"Hey! You brought Luigi."

"I almost didn't, because you two hit it off so well," she said. "A couple families have looked at him. I'm not sure if they were serious, but sometimes they call me the next day to see if a dog is still available."

"So someone might adopt him?"

Franny leaned down to pet Luigi's head. He rolled on his back. She laughed. "His little belly antics have charmed several people. I wouldn't be surprised if one of them calls."

Well, dang. Luke knew the whole point of the shelter was to provide a home for the dogs until they found families. But somehow having Luigi go away didn't sit well with him.

"How much is the adoption fee?"

"Forty-five dollars," Savannah said. "Why?"

Luke jerked his wallet out of his pocket. "I want Luigi. I can't let him go with someone else."

Franny's eyebrows shot up and she turned to Savannah. "Look at that. Luigi had a champion all along."

Savannah waved the money away. "I can't take your money. You've already volunteered so many hours, and I'm sure you will do many more."

"I want it to be official," Luke said. "Do I need to fill out an application? Sign something?"

Savannah passed the Chihuahua to Franny and headed over to the pen where Luigi sat, his big pug eyes staring up at them.

"Are you sure?" Savannah asked.

"T-bone said they used to have a dog out at the RV Park."

"Yes," Savannah said. "Duke. T-bone got him from the shelter. He was a great dog, but already pretty old when T-bone adopted him. He passed on about two years ago."

Luke grinned. "Do you know the history of every animal in Applebottom?"

"If they came through my shelter, I do."

Luke kneeled down to pet Luigi. "I think he and I get along just fine. What you think, Luigi? You want to come home with me?"

Luigi's tongue lolled out and his leg started kicking as Luke rubbed his belly.

"He's overweight," Savannah said. "He needs to be on special food to slim down. And no table scraps. You can't let the people at the RV Park feed him junk."

"I understand," Luke said. "We'll get him all fit and fine."

Savannah glanced over at Franny as if her friend might make the decision for her.

"Don't look at me," Franny said. "I'm just here to help. But I think if a dog can get home, give him a home. It frees up another spot for whatever doggy comes your way tomorrow."

"She's right," Luke said. "And the RV Park should have a new dog."

Savannah nodded. "Okay." She glanced around. "That's not your car though."

"True. I need to come back around for him in my truck. Is that all right?"

"We'll have him ready. There is a little bit of paper-work for the city." She waved her hand at the money that he still held in his fist. "Don't try to pay. It's the least we can do for all the help you've given us."

"All right then," Luke said. "Looks like I just got myself a dog."

Savannah's smile was glorious, and Luke whistled to himself as he gave Luigi one more good scratch then headed back to the car. He'd figured out what was wrong with Mrs. Cole's car. And he got himself a dog. But the smile on Savannah's face – that was what had made this day worthwhile.

Savannah broke down one of the portable fences she'd brought to the adoption event, trying to feel happy for the dogs that had found homes that day.

The shy little girl finally arrived and indeed had fallen in love with Pixie. Tears had sprung to both Savannah's and Franny's eyes when the quivering little Chihuahua settled down on the little girl's lap and laid her head on her arm. Everybody knew that she had found her place.

The couple had come back for Winston after buying some supplies and taken the pit bull home.

And of course, Ollie went early.

Delilah knew all the families personally and could vouch for them, so Savannah didn't even have to be formal about the applications. The only dogs left in her pen were Newton, the big Labrador, and Luigi, who was waiting on Luke.

"You sure he was serious about taking this pug?" Franny asked as they packed up the back of Boone's truck.

"It seems like it," Savannah said. "Maybe he got distracted or delayed."

Soon they were down to just the pen that held Luigi and Newton. Delilah came outside of her shop. "Successful day, girls! I love it when the pups find a home."

"Thank you for giving us the push to do one today," Savannah said. "Did everybody get their starter boxes?"

"They did." Delilah leaned over the short fence to give the two dogs a scratch. "Nobody wanted these guys?"

"Actually, Luke, you know, T-bone's unexpected son -- he wanted to take Luigi but needed to come back for him because he wasn't in his truck."

"You want me to call over to the RV Park and see what's going on?" Delilah asked.

"That would be great," Savannah said. "I don't mind running him over, but I guess I'm not sure if he was serious."

"Did he pay?" Delilah asked. "That's how you know they're serious."

"I didn't want to take his money," Savannah said. "He's done so much for the shelter and he's a huge volunteer."

Delila stood up. "Let me check. The day probably just got away from him."

"I'll leash these two up," Franny said. "Can you break down the fence?"

"In my sleep," Savannah said.

Franny managed the dogs while Savannah swiftly broke down the last fence and loaded it in the truck. When she got back to the sidewalk, Delilah had stepped out again, phone pressed to her ear. "He says he's still waiting on someone to pick up their car. If you can wait a little while, he'll be over, otherwise, he'll run out to the shelter."

"The shelter's fine," Savannah said. "Tell him I'll be out there within half an hour."

Delilah relayed the message and ducked back inside her shop.

"Well, I guess that's it," Franny said. "Just give me a lift back to my car, and we'll call it a day."

Franny talked nonstop on the way back to the shelter, and Savannah struggled to pay attention. Her mind was on the chores she had to get to when she got home.

The cats had to be fed, and the puppies, and dogs she still had. She might be able to skip mucking the yard today since she was down so many dogs. But then there would be Boone to feed, and at some point, Luke would be coming to fetch Luigi.

"You're a thousand miles away," Franny said.

"Just thinking of the afternoon and evening ahead," Savannah said. "I'm sorry I was ignoring you."

"I wasn't saying anything important."

Savannah pulled up to the side of the house. "Sure is going to be quieter with only six dogs, especially since two of them are just tiny pups," she said.

Franny hopped down and opened the back door to let out the dogs. They hadn't bothered to crate them. "I expect you'll get more before too long. It always seems to happen."

"Thank you for your help."

"Love doing it. Have a good evening, though I 'spect you will with Luke coming." Franny gave her a wink and headed to her car.

Savannah walked the dogs around to the back yard to let them run. When she entered the kennel room through the back, the puppies were sleeping, so she passed on to the house to check on Boone.

He still sat in the same spot in front of the television.

"Hey Boone," she said. "You hungry?"

He shook his head for no. There was a cup on the side table by his chair and an empty plate with a smear of red sauce.

Looks like Flo had already fed Boone. Savannah picked up the plate and headed to the kitchen. Sure enough, a note on the table said there was lasagna she could heat up for her own dinner. And Boone seemed in good spirits today.

Savannah was glad for that. She set the cup and plate in the sink and headed to the cat room. She'd get them fed and do a quick litter box sweep, and maybe she could even sit down for a little bit before the evening chores.

She'd lain on the sofa for what seemed like only a moment when headlights pierced the front window. She startled awake, confused.

Boone still watched TV in the half dark.

She paused for a moment, thinking. Had she fed the cats? Yes. Litter box, yes. Puppies, yes. But the dogs were probably still in the back. She needed to bring them in and feed them. She was halfway through her checklist when someone rapped on the door.

It was Luke.

"I'm so sorry I didn't make it back to the Square. It's been a heck of a day."

"Mine, too," she said and stepped aside to let him in.

"I feel really bad that I put you out so late."

"It's fine." She smoothed her hair back, rumpled and sweaty from her nap. She probably looked a fright.

If Luke was tired or strung out from his day, it definitely didn't show. He wore cowboy boots and jeans that fit exactly the way denim should.

"I was just about to heat up some lasagna," she said. "Have you had dinner?"

"I haven't," he said. "I wanted to get right over here since I was so late."

"My aunt made it," she said. "I'll fix you some."

"Can I help with anything out back?"

"I need to feed the dogs," she said. "But I doubt they'll starve."

"How about I give them their evening meal while you heat up the lasagna?"

Having help was the most amazing thing. Savannah could already feel her shoulders relaxing. "That sounds nice."

When Luke had passed through to the kennel room, Savannah poked her head into the living room. "Boone? You hungry yet?"

He waved his arms at her in the way she knew meant he was annoyed that she was interrupting his program. She would check with him again when it was over.

Flo had left more than just a lasagna. There was a nice salad and a fresh pitcher of sweet tea. That woman was a godsend.

When she moved the lasagna tray out, one section already having been removed for Boone, she spotted a hunk of lemon cake. Savannah wanted to swoon. Dessert, too.

She surveyed the shabby kitchen and wondered if it would be too unexpected to light some candles instead of the glaring overhead light. She dug around in a back cabinet and found two candlesticks with white tapers that still had a lot of life left in them. She set them on the table.

But as she sliced the lasagna and arranged salad in bowls, she decided against it. Luke was here to pick up his dog, not have a surprise romantic dinner.

She would stick the lasagna in the microwave, then put the candles away before he noticed.

But Luke came back in, a tiny Rottweiler puppy in each hand. "They are awake and hungry," he said. "I wasn't sure if it was feeding time or not."

Savannah glanced at the table. The candles! Too late now.

"Just like a baby, interrupting a meal," she said with a shaky laugh.

"I'm happy to do it," he said.

"Let me heat up their milk," she said. "We can knock this out before we eat."

"Tom and Jerry and I will just wait here," he said, holding a puppy up on each side of his face. He looked so sweet and adorable, that Savannah felt her blood rush to her head

She hurried to the back to heat up the formula. Hopefully Luke would assume they always had candles on the table. A romantic dinner wasn't in the cards anyway. She just had too much to do.

Luke sat at Savannah's table, both of the squirming puppies in his lap. They were cute little things, their tiny yips barely registering.

The one with the cast on its leg tried to crawl up his chest.

"Hold on there a minute, partner," he said. "We're fetching you your dinner."

Luke didn't know how Savannah did it. Manage the dogs, plus the cats. Adoption days. Random visitors trying to drop off animals they found. And her dad. Plus the normal everyday stuff of having a house.

She boggled his mind.

Jerry wiggled perilously close to the end of Luke's knee, and he picked him up. "Watch where you're going, little buddy. I don't need you taking a nosedive on my watch."

The microwave beeped, and the smell of pasta and tomato sauce filled the kitchen. He hadn't expected to get dinner out of the deal. That meant extra time with Savannah. He glanced at the table. Just two plates set out.

A pair of silver candlesticks sat in the middle of the table. He liked that she took the time to add a little detail to make dinner nice.

Luke lifted the puppies and stood up. There had to be matches around here somewhere.

He circled the kitchen, lightly jiggling the puppies. They stopped yelping and looked around with him, curious about the room.

"Spotted the matches yet? Little box, about the size of your heads."

They had a gas stove, and it looked a little long in the tooth. His mama had a gas stove, and they had to light the burners by hand. It always stressed him out, that moment when she lit the gas and the blue flame flickered to life. He always thought she would get burned. But she didn't.

"Aha," he said, spotting a box of matches half hidden beneath an oven mitt. "Success."

He tucked both puppies against his belly with one arm and picked up the box of matches. He headed back over to the table.

"Don't be squirming off there," he said to them, striking a match on the side of the box. It flared into life, and either the sight of the flame, or the smell, caught both of the dogs' attention. He lit the candles, noting that they smoked a little before catching fire. They hadn't been burned in a while. Interesting.

He waved the match out and set it on top of the box.

He shifted the puppies back to his lap. "Good work, chaps. Mission accomplished."

Savannah entered the kitchen again, a small slender bottle of milk in each hand.

"You lit the candles," she said.

"I thought it was a right nice idea."

She looked at him, then the candles, then the matches. "You're very resourceful."

"Always had to be."

She set the bottles on the table and reached out for the puppy with the cast. "Come here, Tom. Time for dinner."

Savannah tilted the bottle into Tom's mouth. He sucked and chewed on it, gulping the milk.

"We're coming to the end of the hand feeding. They're getting big."

Luke picked up the bottle. The moment he brought it close to the pup in his lap, the little hound snapped his mouth around the end. "Somebody's hungry," Luke said to him.

Savannah stood with Tom and walked over to the microwave. She shifted the pup and the bottle to one hand and pulled the tray of lasagna out with the other. She was obviously used to multitasking.

She brought the tray over to the table and set it down. "The salads are already in bowls."

"Nice," he said. His puppy had already halfway downed his milk. Savannah had been right. They would finish these in no time. "Do we need to take them for a little walk after this?"

"No, they will totally conk out at this hour."

"All the kennel dogs are in their spots with their food, including Luigi."

"You have everything you need for him? I could send you with some dog food, and a water bowl and a leash if you need one."

"Actually, Delilah stopped by the RV Park with all that on her way home. Right nice of her."

"She likes to give a little gift to all the people who adopt dogs."

Tom finished his bottle first. His eyes were closed. Savannah stood up. "I'll go ahead and put them down so I can finish up the dinner."

Luke's little pup was looking droopy as well. He set the bottle on the table. Savannah had told him how she'd come across the abandoned pups. They were lucky.

Savannah returned. "How's Jerry doing?"

"Almost out. I'll take him on back."

When the puppy was all snug next to his sibling, Luke shut the bay and went back to the kitchen.

"I wasn't sure if I should dim the overhead lights," Savannah said. "You lit the candles, but it might be a little dark for a dinner."

"Let me wash my hands and, sure, why not make this a right proper Saturday night?"

Savannah laughed nervously. He wondered what she normally did on weekends. All her days had to be more or less the same. You couldn't sleep in when there were animals to be fed.

Luke spent most of his free time out at the RV Park, usually helping one camper or another who hadn't planned for nighttime, either their electricity not set up correctly, or a light bulb burned out leaving them in the dark.

But the beach by the water was nice. And most nights, at least a few locals would head over and light fires in the pits that were buried in the sand.

Maybe he should ask Savannah if she wanted to go over there one weekend. In fact, he was pretty sure that's exactly what he wanted to do.

He dried his hands on the towel next to the sink and

glanced around for the light switch. "Is this it over here?" he asked, his hand by the main door.

"That'll work," she said.

When the lights went down, his eyes had to adjust to the low flicker of the candles. It was darker than he anticipated.

"I'll have to remember this for when I cook something that isn't as pretty as this," Savannah said, carving out a slice of lasagna for Luke's plate.

He settled in the chair. "Your dad not eating with us?"

"Flo fed him while ago, and he didn't want to be disturbed from a show. I'll check on him again in a bit."

"I don't think I've met anybody named Flo."

"Boone's sister She's a waitress over at Annabelle's Café."

"I've probably seen her, then." Luke stabbed his lasagna and cut off the corner. He was looking forward to this. T-bone didn't make anything for dinner that didn't come off a hibachi grill. "She got kids?"

"Flo used to be married, but they split up something like ten years ago. Their only son died when he was seven. Heart defect."

"That's tough. Any grandparents? Cousins on your mom's side?"

"No, Boone is pretty up there, having met my mom late in life. Both his parents had passed on before I was born. I don't know much about Mom's family other than she ran away when she was sixteen."

Luke had done the same. Tough families were every-where. He swallowed a bite. "This is really good."

"Flo is a great cook. Sometimes when Annabelle is short kitchen staff, she'll help out."

"We need to get her and T-bone together," Luke said. "Then I will eat like a king."

Savannah laughed. "I'm not sure there's very many men in this world who could handle being around Flo for more than an hour. I love her, but she's a tough one."

"And here I thought Gertrude was the only surly bird in town."

"Oh, there's quite a few. You'll get to know them all."

They ate in companionable silence for a while, then Luke asked, "You sad to see those dogs go?"

"No, it's good when they get a home. It was a good day."

"Do you often get rid of that many dogs at once?"

"No. Delilah had just been collecting families who were interested. So we sort of knew at least three would go today."

"Will more come pretty quick?"

"Hard to say. If I don't get any strays or drop-ins this week, I'll call over to a couple other shelters who might be overflowing and see who I can take off their hands."

"So you guys talk to each other."

"Of course. And some of the rescues and foster groups too."

Luke scraped the last bit of lasagna off his plate.

"Sure seems like you could take a lot more animals. There's plenty of kennels."

"I could. But I just can't handle it with Boone. We used to have a lot of volunteers. When we were at full capacity, there were thirty dogs and twenty cats and usually two or three volunteers every day."

"When did it fall off?"

Savannah turned a tomato around in her salad bowl. "About two years ago, when Boone took a real step down in his dementia. Up till then, we could laugh about it, fake it a little bit, and I could smooth things over. But after that, it just didn't work to have a lot of strangers coming in and out of the house."

She kept her eyes downcast, and Luke figured there was more to the story. Maybe more than T-bone knew. Maybe more than anybody knew.

"I really admire how you run this place. It's a lot for anybody to handle."

A cough from the other room made her turn her head toward the door. Luke realized that even if he wanted Savannah to come sit by a fire pit with him, she might not be able to get free.

"So Boone can't be left alone now?"

"He can for short periods. I just don't risk it for long. We're a little isolated on this land. If we were in town and had close neighbors to check on him, it'd be different."

"You ever think of selling and moving into town?"

"I don't think I'm ready to give up the shelter. Not

yet. My dad made it for my mother. As long as he still has good days where he knows what we're doing, I feel like I should keep it."

"But after that?" Luke prodded.

"I don't know. I love running the shelter. I do. I just can't seem to have a life while I'm doing it."

Luke sat back in his chair. The candlelight flickered on Savannah's face. She had to be one of the prettiest girls he'd ever seen. But she seemed worn out, an old soul. And Luke decided right then and there that he was going to find a way to put a little youth back into Savannah Perkins, whether she liked it or not.

CHAPTER 8

*L*uke found little time the following week to act on his decision to help Savannah make her life easier.

Two new dogs arrived at the shelter on Tuesday, one of them a Doberman who had been abused and proved terribly aggressive.

Sergeant didn't take too kindly to the newcomer, and he set all the dogs on edge with his regular admonishment of the Doberman. The new arrival had to be segregated from the other dogs for playtime, and Savannah worked with him as best she could.

As the two of them stood in the main part of the yard, watching the Doberman in the smaller section, snarling and barking through the chain-link fence at the other dogs, Luke asked, "How often do you get dogs like this one?"

"Pretty often. Sometimes, like with this guy, they've been harmed." She shook her head.

"How do you know?"

"He's got scars on his hindquarters," Savannah said. "Doc Black found them."

"I'd like to get my hands on the jerks who treated him so badly." Luke gripped the chilly bar of the fence. How could people do that to animals? "Where did he come from?"

Savannah reached in her pocket and tossed a large treat bone into the Doberman's yard. "He attacked the chickens owned by Mrs. Humphries."

"Who's that?"

"She's a secretary up at the elementary school. She's not what you would call a sweet old lady." Savannah gave him a wan smile. "The way he behaved alarmed her, so she called the sheriff."

"I guess Applebottom doesn't have a dog catcher or animal control?"

Savannah shook her head. "We're the closest thing to that here. And everyone knows that with Boone and the way things are, I can't always just stop and go fetch a dog."

"Maybe if some of those calls come through, I can do it."

"Maybe."

They watched the Doberman lie in a patch of grass with the bone. Now that he was no longer jumping and snarling, he looked like anybody's pet, sleek and black and happily gnawing on a treat.

"He doesn't look like he's been hungry," Luke said.

"I think he got quite a few of the chickens around town."

"He must be smart, then. Which means trainable."

"I'll give it a shot."

Luke took a step back from the fence. "There's another food delivery coming today. I'm going to go move aside the older sacks of feed so that we can establish a good rotation."

Savannah turned to him. "You've only been here a week, and already I don't know how I'd run this place without you"

"I like being here."

"Well, I will enjoy having you as long as you're able. The way Sadie Cole was raving about how you fixed her car tells me that you're going to have a booming repair business very soon. And then I'll lose you."

Luke paused. He felt torn already. He knew his future would change, particularly in the amount of time he could spend out at the shelter. "I won't allow the car business to get too crazy," he said. "If for no other reason than because my major aim is to get back into vet school and finish."

"And where will you go once that's done?"

He shrugged. "No idea. That seems way down the line. For now, though, I will only take the amount of cars I could continue to fix once I start classes again.

Which means that vet school time is reserved for you." He offered her a grin and was rewarded with another smile back, a more genuine one this time.

"I'm grateful. I'll try not to get too used to you."

Luke walked on to the shed. They were little ahead on dog feed, since several had been adopted last weekend. The click of dog nails made him turn around. Luigi had followed him into the shed. The pug flopped on his back for a belly rub.

"You're spoiled, you know that?"

Still, Luke took a moment to give him a good scratch. He'd tried leaving Luigi with T-bone at the RV Park, but the poor dog had taken to chasing up the road after his truck. In the end, he'd started bringing the dog back to the shelter on the days that he came out to volunteer.

Savannah seemed happy to see the dog, particularly after adopting out four at once. If they got too full at the shelter, or it seemed Luigi was causing a problem, he'd figure out a way to get him more attached to T-bone, so he'd be less likely to take off every morning. He wouldn't be able to go with Luke once he started classes anyway.

And about that. There'd been a hang up when he tried to transfer his old vet school credits as he applied for the new one. He was hoping to be in by the spring semester. But that deadline was looming. If this didn't work out soon, he'd definitely be at the shelter for a while. It might be a year before he got back to classes.

He stood up and began shifting the bags of dog food to make room for the new. While he was at it, he rearranged the boxes of cat litter to be less perilously stacked. He unearthed a bag of miscellaneous cat toys that looked to be donated from the accessories wall at Delilah's bakery.

He'd ask Savannah if she wanted to add any new items to the cat room.

When he eventually got to vet school, he'd have to ask around why they weren't volunteering at Savannah's shelter. It might be a forty-five minute drive, but it was a great place to get an all-around picture of what it was like to help these animals.

He'd learned more in a week there than in his classes so far at vet school. He knew he needed the medical piece as well. But for the average little things that might come through a veterinary practice, this by far was the best way to use your extra time, at least until you did a rotation in an actual veterinarian practice.

And Savannah sure needed the help. He rearranged the shed and picked up the bag of cat toys to show Savannah. He'd just shooed Luigi out and closed the door when he heard shouting from the side of the house.

What was that?

He hurried along the pave stones, noticing all the dogs in the main yard congregated in the corner. Sergeant was particularly on edge, his paws up on the chain-link, his low growl suggesting some sort of threat.

Luke clutched the bag and broke out in a run. He pushed his way through the dogs to the gate, making sure he closed it well as all the dogs wanted out.

He rounded the corner of the house, then stopped cold by the overgrown hedge.

Savannah was standing in an angry posture, hands on her hips.

A man about their age leaned against a white Camaro. He had a scruffy beard and dressed pretty typical for a around here in a T-shirt and jeans.

He was as laid-back and chill as Savannah was tense.

"Why not?" the man asked. "Give me one good reason."

Luke was about to intervene when the man reached out and grabbed Savannah's hand in a way that seemed very familiar. Savannah did not shake him off.

Neither of them had noticed him half-hidden by the bush. What should he do? Barrel into the scene? Or back away slowly?

"I think it's a terrible idea," Savannah said. "I'm sure there are a dozen girls you could take instead."

He gave her a snake-oil smile. "But baby doll, I just want it the way it used to be. Anna said you'd be willing. And she's planning to make me a groomsman so you and I can walk down the aisle together. It would be good practice."

Practice? Walking down the aisle? Was Savannah engaged to this man?

Luke took several steps backward. Whatever was making Savannah so stiff, it wasn't keeping her from holding the man's hand. This was just some relationship tiff.

He needed to gracefully exit the situation.

"No," Savannah said. "I know what you did and who you did it with. I'm not interested in being made a fool of again." She jerked her hand away.

Now Luke stopped. He was starting to get a picture of what happened. This was Savannah's ex. And he cheated on her. No, Luke wasn't going to exit the situation gracefully. He would head straight forward.

He walked swiftly up to them. "Is everything okay here?"

"I'm okay," she said. She glanced down at the bag in his hand. "What's that?"

"Looks like Delilah donated some cat toys you forgot about."

The man sneered at him. "This must be the high and mighty Luke. Son of the mayor."

"I am," Luke said. "I volunteer out here the shelter. Funny I haven't seen you around, seeing as Savannah could use the help."

The man's eyes widened. "Now that's a mighty fine idea." He turned to Savannah. "I got time. Need me to help feed the dogs?"

"No," Savannah said, shooting Luke an angry look. "Luke and I have it well under control."

"Luke and I," the man said with a sneer. *Luke and I. Isn't that cozy?*"

Savannah let out a disgusted snort. "Luke, this is Billy Ray. He was just leaving."

Billy Ray turned to his car. "I'm not sure I'm interested in making his acquaintance. But that's a mighty fine idea you have there, Lukey boy. Should I come back tomorrow?"

"No, thank you," Savannah said.

"But Lukey boy here said you needed help."

"*We* have it under control," Luke said. "I only meant to point out that it was interesting that a man with so much *leisure time* hadn't bothered to help out."

"I'm just now back in town," Billy Ray said. He winked at Savannah. "You give a thought to what I said. Sure would love to escort you at the wedding. I think the bride's counting on it."

"I'm quite sure she's not," Savannah turned to Luke. "Come on. Let's go look at these cat toys."

Savannah took the bag and headed toward the gate. But Luke stayed. He stood there, his feet apart, his arms crossed over his chest, until Billy Ray fired up the Camaro and backed down the dirt driveway.

Luke was pretty sure they hadn't seen the last of him.

CHAPTER 9

Savannah found herself riled up all over again about Anna's interference with Billy Ray as she drove Boone's old pickup from Applebottom into Branson.

Today was the final fitting of her bridesmaid dress for the wedding, and based on the text messages she'd been receiving from the other girls, Anna was in a mood.

Well, so was *she*.

Savannah didn't have much time for friends, not anymore. She'd actually been a little surprised when Anna asked her to be a bridesmaid.

But the four of them in the wedding party had been friends since childhood.

Violet was in grad school but was driving back for the fitting. Savannah would be happy to see her.

Candace was still around Applebottom, as she

taught at the elementary. No doubt she would be complaining a mile a minute that she'd been paired with Deputy Jeremy Banks as a groomsman. He was her ex.

Anna herself had never left Applebottom, doing some online college while she waited for her boyfriend Landon to finish his degree. She used to help Savannah out at the shelter, but like so many others, slowed down her visits as Boone got harder to be around.

Flo had taken the day off from the café to watch Boone. She'd have to do it again next weekend for the wedding. Savannah worried she was taking too much of her aunt's time, but what else could she do? Not just anybody could wait on Boone.

She pulled up in front of the boutique. Boone's truck looked terribly out of place parked along the curb with cute little sports cars on either side of it. But Savannah could only shrug it off. She was a blue-collar working girl. She looked down at her hands as she walked up to the boutique door. She needed a manicure or something before next Saturday. She had the fingernails of a farmer.

When she entered the dress shop to the tinkle of a little bell, she spotted Anna right away. This was the sort of shop that fawned over a bride, sitting her in a fancy chair and making sure she had sparkling water and a cluster of salespeople.

Savannah plunked down in the chair beside her. "Am I the first one here?"

"Candace is already back there trying on her dress."

A saleswoman approached in an ivory sheath that looked fancier than anything that Savannah had ever owned. And this woman wore it as part of her *job*.

"This must be Savannah," she said. "I have your dress all ready to try on."

Savannah rubbed her sweaty palms on her jeans. She really should have worn a skirt. She had a couple somewhere. The occasion to break them out was so rare that they generally got buried in the back of her closet. She'd put on a pretty sweater at least. Still, Anna wore a fancy silk shirt and matching pants. And of course, Candace would be dressed to the hilt as always. She prayed Violet would not be too crazy.

"Do come out here so that we can see it," Anna said.

"Okay."

Savannah glanced around anxiously as the saleswoman led her to the back. Everyone here was dressed super cute. She wanted to smack herself on the head for looking so hick.

This whole life was foreign to her. When she closed her eyes at night, all she saw was wagging tails, kennel doors, bags of feed, and of course the never-ending cleanup. Shovel, dirt, poop.

The woman led her through the dressing room to a door with her name written on a whiteboard. "Let me know if you need any help."

Savannah sat on a bench at the back of the stall. How had she ended up in this mess? She was going to look so out of place at Anna's wedding.

She stood up and kicked off her boots. Couldn't she have worn some flats? Something pretty? No, in her rush to get out the door, she had put on her work boots.

She shimmied out of her jeans and pulled her sweater over her head. She almost snort-laughed when she realized she had on an oversized athletic bra. She really hadn't thought this through.

The dress was truly lovely, but it had sheer shoulders and sleeves above the neckline. So Savannah's options were to go out into the main dressing area showing off the bulky extra wide straps of a running bra through the delicate peach lace. Or not wear a bra at all.

How did she get into these predicaments?

She tried pulling her arms out and tucking the straps down into the main bra.

But when she tried on the dress, it looked bulky and strange from the extra fabric.

"Why?" she asked. "Why are you so stupid?"

"Who's stupid?" The voice was so familiar that Savannah almost melted into the floor with relief.

"Violet? It's Savannah."

"I know. I could hear you."

"I forgot to bring a strapless bra."

Violet started to giggle. "You gonna just go without?"

"I can't do that!"

"Why not? You're still perky."

"Can I borrow yours?"

"Really?"

"We're about the same size!"

"Okay, fine."

A bra sailed over the wall between them and landed on the bench.

"You go out first, then bring it back to me," Violet said.

"Oh, thank you. Thank you for saving my life."

"Drama!"

Savannah swiftly lowered the dress, whipped off the athletic bra, and fastened Violet's. When she pulled on the dress, she couldn't quite zip the entire thing in the back, but the salesperson could help with that.

She turned to the mirror on the back wall. Despite her black woolen socks and her messy braid, she didn't look half bad.

On impulse, she yanked the band off the bottom of the braid and rolled it onto her wrist. With a few quick swipes of her fingers, the braid worked loose, and her long brown hair tumbled around her face in loose waves.

Savannah grabbed the bangs section and quickly braided it into a half-crown that circled her head, leaving the rest down. She tied it off with the band and took a deep breath. She was presentable now, even with the thick wool socks.

Anna and the salespeople clapped as Savannah approached them in the main part of the shop. Candace was out there as well, her matching peach dress fitting her like a dream.

"Oh, somebody zip it up the rest of the way," Anna said, lifting her glass of sparkling water.

One of the women shifted Savannah's hair aside and fastened the dress. "Did you forget your shoes? We should be checking the length."

Savannah's face flushed hot. "I forgot them."

Candace kicked hers off. "Here's mine. They're so big that anyone can wear them. Even in your socks."

Her voice had that usual flat Candace quality. Candace had always hated her big feet. But then, Candace hated most things.

"Thank you," Savannah said. Her friends were saving her today.

She slid the shoes on, and they did indeed fit even with the thick socks. She turned in a circle for Anna, who pronounced her perfect.

She handed the shoes back to Candace. "I'm going to run back and check on Violet," she said.

She hoped Anna didn't want to see the three brides-maids together, because it was not going to happen today.

The girls reconvened at a restaurant a couple blocks down from the dress shop.

When they'd ordered, Anna leaned forward against the table, her red hair falling over her shoulders. "Okay,

Savannah. Out with it. Why aren't you coming to my wedding with Billy Ray?"

There it was. She'd been waiting for this moment all afternoon.

Savannah decided to just let the truth fly. Clearly it was time. "Billy Ray cheated on me with that girl from Blue Eye. It went on for months without me even knowing."

Anna held up a hand. "I know."

Wait. What? "How do you know?" Savannah blushed at the shocked looks from her friends. She hadn't told anyone. It was too humiliating.

"He told me," Anna said. "And he's sorry. He was so downtrodden the other night when Landon and I had them over."

"You asked Billy Ray over?" What had been going on with them while she was stuck out at the shelter?

"He just came over for some barbecue."

Candace sat back in her chair, her perfect black hair swinging behind her shoulders. "Anna, just stop. Don't force Savannah to walk with that creep. You've been trying to make me go with Jeremy Banks, and I'm not doing that either."

Violet agreed. "Anna, you've got to let this go."

Anna slammed her hand down on the table, causing all the dishes to rattle. "Girls! You know that Landon's best pals can't make it down for the wedding. So we're struggling with the groomsmen situation."

"The wedding is in a week," Candace said. "You

should have settled the groomsmen situation three months ago."

"Well, Billy Ray and Jeremy are taking Landon out for his stag night," Anna said. "That makes them groomsmen to us."

Savannah fiddled with her napkin. She didn't want to upset Anna, but this matchmaking was not going to happen. "You can have Billy Ray and Jeremy as grooms- men. But that doesn't mean Candace and I have to actu- ally show up with them as dates."

Anna's face pinched like she might cry. "It's not like either one of you have somebody to bring otherwise. It's not gonna hurt you for one night to sit beside these men you used to love and be happy at my wedding."

Candace's mouth flattened in a tight line. She looked like she was about to blow. Violet looked down at her hands. She never was very confrontational.

Savannah would have to be the one to handle this.

"Anna. We're happy to sit with Jeremy and Billy Ray at the tables. But that doesn't mean that they are our dates. We will go to the reception and take our pictures with them. We will smile, and we will do the first dance."

"I'll dance with Billy Ray," Candace said quickly. "Savannah can dance with Jeremy."

"You should dance with your dates!" Anna whined.

"They are not our dates," Candace insisted. "And it's not very fair of you to insist on it. I've never even been to a wedding where the bridesmaids and groomsman were actual couples."

Anna lifted her napkin to her nose. "That's what made it so romantic."

"For you, maybe!" Candace snapped. "For us, it's a nightmare."

"The best man's already married," Violet said. "It's not like he's going to be *my* date."

Anna hid her face.

Savannah sighed. "We don't want these boys to think that we're there to get handsy with, or to kiss under the lights. Any of that."

"Billy Ray will totally get handsy," Candace said. "You have to spare Savannah."

"We're gonna do this right for you," Savannah said. "You don't have to worry about that part."

Anna sniffed again. "Well, all right. If that's how it has to be."

"It is," Candace said sharply.

The waitress brought them their orders, and the conversation turned elsewhere. Savannah felt some relief. Billy Ray could be hard to handle. He was insistent, pushy, and sometimes downright mean.

She wished he hadn't been made a groomsman.

Anna stuck a fork in her salad. "Of course I have a seat for Boone if he can make it. I wouldn't want to leave him out."

"That's really sweet of you," Savannah said.

"No, I mean it. Boone was like a second dad to me.

We spent a lot of time at your shelter when we were kids."

"We did," Candace said.

Savannah looked at her friend, all perfectly dressed and made up. The two of them couldn't be more different now, even though, growing up, they'd all been happy to sit in the dirt with the puppy dogs.

She didn't want to upset Anna now by saying that there was no way Boone could make it. The empty chair was something the bride probably wouldn't even notice on the big day.

That would be for Savannah to wish were different.

CHAPTER 10

*L*uke admitted to feeling dog tired as he pulled his truck onto the highway after leaving a full day at Savannah's shelter.

A lady had brought in three feral cats she had trapped, and despite both him and Savannah wearing special gloves that went up to their elbows, they were the little worse for wear after trying to check the cats for fleas and ticks.

Two more dogs had come in over the weekend, and they'd had to be bathed and rid of fleas as well.

He was only a few miles down the road when he reached over to pet Luigi and realized the dog wasn't there.

Unbelievable. He'd left Luigi in the backyard with the others.

He pulled off the road and turned around. He could probably go to the back of the house and grab the dog without disturbing Savannah or Boone, who were bound to be making dinner by now.

Sometimes Luke stayed for the evening meal, but tonight T-bone was hosting a cookout at the RV Park.

His father would want an update about Luke's plans. He was still fighting the veterinary school about transferring his credits. Turns out his old school's program was unique, and the classes didn't align. And the two states had different qualifications and requirements.

Soon Luke would have to make a hard decision about losing a big chunk of the two years he'd already done to start over in Applebottom, or maybe hightailing it back to Montana to finish.

Maybe he shouldn't have left after his mom died. But the opportunity to meet his father, to have family again, had been a huge draw.

When he pulled up to the shelter, his jaw clamped down to see a white Camaro sitting in the dirt driveway.

Billy Ray. He had no idea what Savannah ever saw in that boy. Luke definitely knew trouble when he saw it. He'd spent half his life *being* the trouble.

Still, Savannah might've invited him over. He didn't want to interrupt. Hopefully he could get his dog from the back and they would be none the wiser.

He didn't like it, though. Not one bit. The idea that Savannah might be sweet on somebody like Billy Ray didn't sit well with him. If she was going to take up with him again, Luke wasn't sure if he could stand it. Maybe he *should* cruise back to Montana. Billy Ray could be what tipped the scales.

He pulled up nice and slow and parked beside the Camaro. He eased his door open, but didn't close it all the way to avoid a big thud that might be heard inside.

He walked quickly around the side of the house to the gate. The chorus of barks and shuffles approaching the corner told him that the dogs were still in the backyard. Good. He could get Luigi and sneak back out again and no one would be the wiser.

He leaned against the fence and looked through the dogs that were piling over each other to get to him.

But Luigi wasn't with them.

Shoot. What should he do?

Savannah came around the corner of the house. "What are you dogs –" she stopped short when she saw Luke. "Is everything okay?"

"I realized Luigi wasn't in my truck," Luke said. "But he's not with the dogs."

"He's by the back door."

She seemed disgusted. Luke didn't know who with. Him? Billy Ray? Something else? He followed her around the side of the house. Luke's fickle dog was lying on his back, belly up, getting scratched by none other than Billy Ray.

The man looked up, frowning when he spotted Luke. "What are you doing back?"

So he'd been waiting for Luke to leave to pop in on Savannah.

"Just fetching my dog," Luke said.

"This one's yours?"

"He adopted him," Savannah said. "And Billy Ray was just leaving." Anger poured off her like hot lava.

"Now, honey darlin'," Billy Ray said. "You know you gotta give me a chance to change your mind."

"Nope," Savannah said. "And I need to see to Boone."

"Let me take you to dinner," Billy Ray said.

"Not happening," Savannah said. She had a hand on her hip and her voice could have cut glass.

Luke had heard enough. "Seems like the lady's told you 'no' more than once," he said. Now that he knew Billy Ray wasn't wanted, he wasn't leaving until the man was gone.

"This isn't any of your beeswax," Billy Ray said. "You take your dog and get on out of here."

"I don't think I will," Luke said.

"It's okay, Luke," Savannah said. "I can handle Billy Ray."

Now Luke was torn. Did he listen to Savannah, or did he deal with Billy Ray?

Billy Ray put his arm around Savannah's shoulders. "You see, Savannah here and I are going to be a couple at Anna's wedding next weekend, aren't we baby doll?"

Savannah closed her eyes, and Luke could tell she was trying to hold her temper.

"Doesn't look like the lady's interested," Luke said.

"Now see, there's something you don't understand," Billy Ray said with a sneer. "Savannah and I have a history. Something you wouldn't know nothing about. And we are meant to be."

"Billy Ray—" Now Savannah sounded annoyed.

"You need to hear it, sugar plum. This wedding where you're a bridesmaid and I'm a groomsman is our great opportunity to show the world we were meant to walk the aisle side-by-side." He held out his arm as if the picture of it was in front of them.

Savannah let out a little groan. "Billy Ray, I already told you. Just because we're both in the wedding doesn't mean we have to go together."

"Sure it does, baby doll," he said. "It's like it was written in the stars."

Luke tried to keep his annoyance in check. "I hate to break it to you, Billy *Bob*," he said. "But Savannah can't go to the wedding with you."

Billy Ray laughed and kicked at the dirt, sending a spray near the dogs. They backed off with a series of yelps.

That was it. Luke grabbed the man's hand and slung it off Savannah. He whistled for his dog, and for once, Luigi jumped up and stood beside him.

Billy Ray narrowed his eyes at Luke. "You're going to regret doing that."

"I doubt it," he said. "Savannah's being nice, but she can't go to the wedding with you," he said. He was about to say the boldest lie he'd told in a long time.

Billy Ray crossed his arms over his measly chest. "And why's that?"

Luke took his time fastening a leash to Luigi's collar, holding them all in suspense. Even Savannah looked at him curiously.

But when Luke stood up, he gave them a big ol' grin. This wasn't going to go over well, but he was doing it anyway.

"Because she's already agreed to go to the wedding with *me*."

When Billy Ray threw a punch at Luke, Savannah's first concern was for the dogs.

She ran a couple steps away and called to the dogs so they would come up to the back of the house. If those two boys wanted to be idiots and get in a fight, she didn't want to have anything to do with either one of them.

When all the dogs were inside the kennel room, she turned to see that Billy Ray was continuing to swing wildly at Luke, who simply smiled and ducked beneath each shot. It looked like some strange sort of dance, Billy Ray's arm swinging wide, and Luke, with a big wide grin, spinning out of his way.

"Get over here and take a punch like a man!" Billy Ray said.

Luke just laughed. "I will if you start swinging like one."

Savannah had had enough. "Billy Ray, knock it off

and just leave." She closed the back door and pulled her cell phone out of her pocket. "I'm serious. I'm about to call Jeremy to arrest you."

"Jeremy won't do diddly squat to me," Billy Ray said, keeping his eyes on Luke so he could take another swing. "We were classmates, and he's in the wedding too. We had a right good time at the stag party."

Savannah wanted to scream. Dust flew up from where the two men circled each other. It looked like a game for Luke, who smiled the whole time, his boots shuffling in the yard.

"Then I'm calling Officer Stone."

The tones beeped loudly as she dialed. Billy Ray stopped throwing punches and turned to look at her. "You seriously calling the cops?"

Savannah subtly canceled the call but put the phone up to her ear anyway. "You bet I am. I can't have this ridiculousness in my backyard. You're scaring the dogs."

Savannah continued to fake the call. "Brenda? Can you send Officer Stone out to the shelter? Billy Ray is acting the fool, and I'm about to get his butt arrested."

Billy Ray's eyes got big. "You did not just call the dispatch."

"You bet I did."

"Well, shoot." He glared at Luke. "This ain't over, buddy."

"Good. I need the cardio."

Billy Ray stomped over to the gate and pushed

through, not bothering to close it. Thank goodness the dogs were inside.

When he was gone, Savannah stuck the phone back in her pocket.

"Did you just fake that call?" Luke asked.

"Maybe."

"You had us both fooled."

Savannah put her hand on the door. "Well, that was the intention."

"You really going to go to the wedding with that guy?"

"No. But he is going to make it really terrible. It's all anybody would talk about the bridesmaid luncheon last weekend."

"Let me go close the gate."

Savannah watched him hurry over and shut the gate. Why did this have to be so complicated? And why had Billy Ray come back?

The way he panicked by her threat to call Officer Stone, Savannah had a feeling Billy may have racked up some priors. He was a hotheaded thing, and always had been. It had been sort of amusing, though, to see him trying to hit Luke and fail.

When Luke came back around, the two of them walked inside the kennel room. The dogs were milling around, lost without the structure of feed bowls or bedtime.

"Want me to help them get kenneled up?" Luke asked.

"No, you need to get to that cookout."

Luke found Luigi and picked up the leash from the floor. "You sure he won't come back?"

"I'm sure."

"At least let me go get the Doberman from the small yard."

"All right."

When Luke returned with Nero, he started kenneling the dogs even though Savannah had told him to go. Savannah let him. When everyone except Luigi was kenneled up, she said, "Thanks for not actually fighting with him."

Luke ran his hand over his jaw. "Can't let him destroy my modeling career."

Savannah busted out laughing so hard that she had to hold her belly. All the tension from the altercation drained away.

"How did this happen?" she asked between giggles.

"Every small town has its hothead or five."

"Billy Ray's enough trouble for five."

"You really dated him?" Luke leaned against the line of kennels, crossing one ankle over the other.

"It was years ago. Before things went so downhill. I was younger and had a lot less to worry about."

Oh, to be young and stupid enough to date somebody like Billy Ray. She almost missed it, well, not Billy Ray himself. But being impulsive. Heading off with some cute guy just because he was into you.

Back then, it hadn't mattered so much if she didn't

think everything through. Boone ran the shelter and she just helped. She could afford to make a mistake like Billy Ray. Not now.

"I was serious about the wedding." Luke reached down to scratch Luigi's head. "Sounds like you might need someone to help you run interference."

The puppies were stirring, so Savannah walked over to the sick bay and picked up Jerry. She pressed the little pup to her neck. "I don't know. That might antagonize him."

"Better to antagonize him while you have someone there solely to watch your back, than to do it on your own without help. Weddings are emotional. It makes people do stupid things."

"It's this weekend," Savannah said. "I'm sure you already have plans."

"Naw," he said. "Anyhow, this sounds way more interesting than anything I might have going."

Savannah smoothed the puppy dog's ears. It would be nice to have someone watching out for her while she was at the wedding. Luke had proven he could handle Billy Ray without actually getting in a fight. That was more than she could say for most of the men she knew.

"All right," she said. "Let's do it. Besides, if I don't, he'll think I've given in."

"Good. It's settled." Luke led Luigi to the back door. "But I do worry about you. Guys like that can be big-time bad news."

She had no answer to that. Luke headed across the

back yard, and Savannah latched the door. If Billy Ray was going to come around and cause trouble, she'd need to be more careful about locking things up. She hated that. And she hated that the young and foolish version of her had ever given Billy Ray the time day.

She turned back to the sick bay to set down Jerry and mix a little softened food. It was time to feed these babies.

And somehow, she had herself a date to Anna's wedding.

CHAPTER 11

Savannah turned in front of the mirror for the twentieth time. She hadn't looked like this in a couple of years at least.

She might only be twenty-four, but she sure felt older. It was that hard period with Boone that did it. Losing the volunteers. Worrying about how she could continue to care for her father. Billy Ray cheating on her.

But not today. Violet had come over that morning and done her nails and helped with makeup. They had a long day ahead, so they needed armor, Violet had said. Armor by Maybelline.

All the families were close. Seeing them again would be nice, something normal after so much hardship. She sure wished Boone could go, but there was no way. Even though he was having a good morning, there was no guarantee that he wouldn't fall apart later. As a bridesmaid, Savannah had a lot of responsibilities. If Boone got confused or out of control, Savannah would be stuck.

She shoved it from her mind and tweaked one of the curls near her ear.

No, today she was one of those days you could look forward to.

Billy Ray had left her alone. And something between Savannah and Luke had shifted since the night Bully Ray tried to start a fight.

They smiled at each other a lot more, like they had a secret between them. Well, she guessed they did. Everybody needed to think that them going to the wedding was the real thing, when really it was just an arrangement to keep Billy Ray away from her.

Still, it was sort of fun to be in on something with Luke. He'd been nothing but helpful to her, kind and charming, and full of good ideas. She wished there was something she could do for him, but unfortunately, her calling the vet school on his behalf would probably do more harm than good.

She twirled in the dress one more time, then heard a car crunching on the dirt driveway outside. She ran to the window and looked down. It was Luke. He'd decided he needed to go early just like her, since Billy Ray would be there. Having him around would certainly make their fake relationship look more legitimate. Who else but a devoted boyfriend would stick around for hours of pre-wedding boredom?

She hurried down the hall and popped into the kitchen. Flo was there, washing dishes in the sink. Flo was good like that, always helping out when she came.

"I'm about to leave," she said.

Flo turned around, her eyes lighting up when she saw Savannah. "Why don't you just look like a ray of sunshine."

"Thank you," Savannah said. "I haven't worn a dress in years."

"You should do it more. Is Violet taking you out there?"

Savannah hesitated. If Flo didn't know about Luke, that meant people weren't talking about it in town. Any number of people would have mentioned it to her at the café.

Which meant Billy Ray had kept his mouth shut for once. Interesting.

"No, it's Luke, the one who's been helping me out around the shelter."

"The mayor's son?" Flo dried her hands on a dish towel. "It's going as well as that?"

"He's super great. Super helpful." Savannah felt stuck. She couldn't let her aunt think they were actually dating, but she didn't want Flo to let it slip at the café that they were faking it to thwart Billy Ray.

She was saved by Luke's knock, which sent several of the dogs in the back to barking. "I'll go handle them," Flo said. "Don't you worry about the evening feed."

"Thank you so much. It's a huge job."

Flo waved her hand. "Don't worry about it, baby girl. You just have yourself a nice time at Anna's wedding."

Flo headed to the kennels.

By the time Savannah made it to the living room, Boone had already gotten up to open the front door. When Boone saw Luke in a suit, he held up his hand and said, "We already got plenty of Jesus in this house. But thank you."

Savannah took Boone by the hand. "Boone, this is Luke. Remember, he helps us in the shelter with the dogs?"

Boone's thick gray eyebrows drew together. "Oh, right. Luke. With the dogs. Come on in. You're dressed mighty nice."

"Thank you, sir," Luke said. He glanced at Savannah to get a clue as to how she wanted him to handle Boone today.

Over the weeks that Luke had been working with her, they'd created a simple nonverbal communication about Boone. The *you might want to stay out of his way, he's angry* look. The *he's really confused, so just smile and nod* look.

But when Luke's eyes landed on her, all the thoughts of how she might want to address Boone today flew out of her mind. He swallowed hard, the Adam's apple in his throat working up and down.

Savannah felt a flush creep over her body. Nobody had stared at her like that in a long time. Maybe not even Billy Ray.

"You look so beautiful," Luke said.

This caught Boone's attention. He glanced from Luke to Savannah and back to Luke again. "Are you taking my daughter on a date?" Boone asked.

"I'm taking her to Anna's wedding, sir," Luke said.

Boone nodded, his eyes searching the floor as if the answer could be read there. "A wedding. That's mighty fine."

Then something seemed to dawn on him and he bounced on his feet. "A wedding! Finally!" He turned to Savannah. "And you make a most beautiful bride!"

Savannah's mouth went dry. She wasn't sure how to correct him or if he would even understand. If his emotions got this high, they could easily turn belligerent, and then Flo would have a hard time.

Finally, she just said, "Thank you, Boone."

Boone leaned forward to shake Luke's hand. "I'm so happy to know that Savannah is taken care of," he said. "That's been on my mind a lot lately. I sure am glad for it." The shake became fierce, pumping up and down for long moments.

But Luke just kept the same easy smile. "Thank you, sir."

Savannah's stomach dropped. Boone worried about her? He wanted her married?

Boone finally released Luke's hand. "Well, you lovebirds better get to it. Can't keep the preacher man waiting. Nothing more romantic than two people running off to get married. That's what me and Savannah's mother did."

Savannah bit the inside of her cheek to keep her eyes from pricking. She reached for her bag. "He's right, Luke. We should go."

Flo came back into the living room as they approached the door. "You guys have a good time."

Boone turned to her sister. "Did you know they were getting married? Best news I've had all year."

Flo understood the situation. She took Boone's arm and led him back to his chair. "I heard. Isn't that just lovely?"

As they got settled, Savannah and Luke headed out the front door. She still felt a little shook up as they got into the truck.

When they were headed down the highway, Luke said, "That's got to be really tough."

Savannah watched the landscape slide by. "I didn't want to upset him right before we left by telling him he was wrong. But I'll tell him tomorrow."

"Okay, good," Luke said. "I don't want to fool him. But I understand."

"He may not even remember," Savannah said. "Don't worry."

"You really do look beautiful," Luke said. "It's not right, outshining the bride like you will."

Savannah to him. "You look pretty smart yourself. I hate that you're going to be stuck there for so many hours."

"I'll find something to do," he said. "It's been a spell since I've been to a wedding. I'm just going for the cake."

That was so Luke, always making it seem like some big favor wasn't any trouble at all. Savannah was grateful for him and vowed that she would do something to help him the way he had helped her.

*

Luke had never been to a wedding where he didn't know anyone, not even the bride.

He didn't often find himself in situations like this, though, so he rolled with the novelty of it and tried to make himself useful.

Savannah had disappeared immediately into the bowels of the church to help the bride get dressed. Initially, Luke sat on a pew situated in the entryway.

A rather harried woman had entered the space trying to drag a large folding table while wearing a floral dress and low heels. Luke jumped up immediately to carry the table.

"Where do you want it?" he asked.

"Near the door. It's for the guestbook and a place for people who bring gifts to the ceremony instead of the reception."

He set the table on its side, pulling down the legs and locking them in place. When it was situated where the woman wanted, they covered it with a tablecloth.

"Thank you," the woman said. "Do I know you?"

Luke extended a hand. "I'm Luke Southard. I came with Savannah, one of the bridesmaids."

"Oh, how lovely. Savannah is such a sweet girl," the woman said. She straightened a long necklace of clear beads across her chest. "I'm Felicia Morrow, Anna's aunt. I'm helping with the setup."

"I'm at your disposal until the wedding begins," Luke said. "I know Savannah will be quite busy getting prepared and taking photographs."

"Aren't you a doll," Alicia said. "Come to my car. Carrying boxes is much quicker with a strong young man."

And just like that, Luke became a part of the proceedings. He unloaded boxes. Carried flower arrangements. Set out photographs of the bride and groom, pausing at the image of Savannah as a young girl sitting in her own backyard with a bunch of puppy dogs, alongside the other girls who ended up in the bridal party.

What a nice thing to have friends your whole life. Luke and his mother had moved around quite a lot in his early years. Mom had never really succeeded anywhere, and often they took off to avoid bills or eviction or an unruly ex.

Luke could scarcely remember the name of anyone he played with as a child. Funny the things that made you lucky in life. It often had nothing to do with the kind of car you drove or the size of your house. Little things, like friends you'd known since you were five.

"Oh, Luke!" Felicia called. "The girls would love it if you would carry the bouquets while they take pictures without them."

He liked this. He'd get to see Savannah with her friends.

He followed Felicia down a set of stairs where the church must hold Sunday school, as each door had a sign with a set of ages for the children.

Felicia led him to a door marked *nursery*.

A couple of girls sat in rocking chairs, watching the bride, who posed for the photographer in front of a large window with white curtains.

He scanned the room for Savannah but didn't see her.

Felicia led him to a box filled with flowers. "Each bouquet is in a little jug of water," she said. "If you take them out, they need to be dried off or you'll get water spots on your clothes." She tucked a hand towel in the corner.

Luke gave her a quick nod to show he understood. He accepted the box and waited for further instructions.

A door opened from a tiny room in the back, and Savannah emerged. She stopped short when she saw him. "Luke!" She glanced at the box in his hands. "Glad you found something to do."

"Oh, he has been such a doll. Helping all over the place." Felicia fluttered over to Savannah, adjusting her dress, and straightening a little pin that was fastened over her heart. That was new. Probably a gift from the bride, as all the bridesmaids had them.

A photographer instructed the bride to shift her face in the light from the window and snapped a series of shots. Then the bridesmaids were arranged around her. As they worked, Luke began to pick the girls apart. Candace was tall, with straight black hair and an expression that always made it seem like she'd rather be somewhere else, even when she smiled.

Violet was silly and fun, cracking jokes that only the girls seemed to understand. They all wore peach dresses with lacy tops, but in his opinion, Savannah wore it best.

"Do you want the bouquets?" Felicia asked the photographer.

"Not until the formal pictures," he said.

As they made their way up the stairs to the main level of the church, Felicia came up behind him. "Luke, can you make sure that the groom and groomsmen are nowhere in sight? We can't have him seeing the bride before the ceremony."

Luke hesitated, not wanting to admit that he had no clue what the groom looked like, but then he remembered that he did know Billy Ray, and it might be amusing to bump into him this way.

He moved out beyond the last step and looked around. A few more people had gathered, almost exclusively older women in variations of the same style of flowered dress. He turned back to Felicia. "No man on this level currently," he said.

"Okay, girls," Felicia said.

They hurried inside the sanctuary and walked down the aisle. A white arch had been constructed at the front, covered in peach and white flowers. The photographer arranged the women around it and took another series of pictures. Finally, he said, I'm going to go to the groom now. I'll be back when Anna's father comes to fetch her."

"Should we put our bouquets back in water?" Violet asked Felicia.

"Give them back to Luke," Felicia said. "We want them to stay fresh."

Luke lowered his box so that each girl could place her bouquet inside. Anna and the other bridesmaids hurried back down the stairs to their hidden room, but Savannah held back to walk with Luke. "Everything going okay? I'm sorry it's such a long wait. I could've driven myself."

"No, I don't mind. It's been sort of fun meeting people who know you outside of the shelter."

Savannah grinned up at him, and the glow in his chest fired up again. "Has everything been okay so far?" he asked.

"Perfect. The groomsmen aren't allowed anywhere near us so it's just been us friends."

"It must be nice."

"I'm pretty much free now. Anna's parents will take

over, and we won't be expected to be near her until about fifteen minutes before the ceremony."

"Then I say let's drop this box off with the others and take a look around," Luke said.

So they did, leaving the box in Violet's care and heading back up the stairs. They walked outside, where the early fall day shone bright and clear.

Cars were starting to arrive, the early birds who probably worried about being late.

"Where's the reception?" Luke asked.

"A little hall on the other side of town," Savannah said.

"Will you ride with me?"

"Yes. They only got a limo for the bride and groom."

She led him down a concrete path. Luke could see the gardens just ahead. A spiral of hedges led to a flower garden.

"This is nice," he said.

They made it to the very center of the garden and sat on a little concrete bench.

"Sometimes I wish I could make a flower garden on the land beyond the dog yards," Savannah said. "When I was little, I would plant flowers here and there, just outside the fence. But there never seems to be enough time."

"I think we make time for the things that are important to us," Luke said.

"Well, unless I can add another hour to every day, I won't be adding a flower garden to my daily duties."

"I'm surprised you don't have more volunteers. When I was up at the veterinary school in Montana, all of us were expected to put in quite a few hours at clinics and shelters."

Savannah looked down at her hands. "We did. But Boone caused some issues and the school took us off the list."

"Can you get back on?"

"Not likely. I get some help around town, people who've known Boone for years. Like Franny, who came to adoption day. And there are a few others. Gayle, who you haven't met. And sometimes Jesse comes."

"That's not a lot of respite for you."

Savannah shrugged. "I manage."

Luke decided to let it go. He didn't want to ruin the happy day with hard conversation. Across from them, an explosion of blooms in a tiered concrete planter was the centerpiece of the garden.

"So which of those flowers are your favorite?" he asked.

"The anemones, I'd say. They're so red, like jewels."

"They do stand out. Are those others daisies?"

"Yes. They are small but they have a lot of color."

"And roses bloom in the fall?"

"Lots of flowers do, if they're cared for properly."

Savannah stood and leaned closer to the flowers, her hand cupping a bright red blossom. Luke wanted to freeze the moment of her standing there, backed by so much riotous color, looking as beautiful as any girl he'd ever seen.

"I'm glad I came with you," he said.

She smiled over at him. "Even as a fake date?"

"Is it?" He left the bench to come nearer to her. "This feels pretty real." His heart pounded in his ears. He was taking a terrible risk. If she thought he was being too pushy, he could spoil everything.

But she looked up at him, and in this light, with them so close, he could see little gold specks dancing in her warm brown eyes.

"It does," she said, and her voice was so soft, and her gaze so easy, that he knew she felt like he did. That this was right. They worked well together, side by side. And now he could feel something else sparking through him, lighting a path to his heart like a fuse.

He reached for her hand, and she let him, their fingers entwining. They kept staring at each other, and he thought he might lean in, learn the softness of her lips, when the bells at the top of the church began to peel.

"Oh no," she said. "I'm late!"

She released him and they hurried toward the church in a mad dash.

CHAPTER 12

The ceremony itself was lovely. Savannah enjoyed standing at the front of the church, watching her childhood friend marry the man of her dreams.

She felt Billy Ray's eyes on her throughout the service. The bridesmaids were angled toward the couple, so it was easy for him to snag her attention. He winked at her at least a dozen times, setting off an internal groan with each one.

Thankfully, the bride was in a happy glow, because she hadn't noticed that the groomsmen, who probably hadn't paid that much attention to these details, were not standing in the right order for Billy Ray to pair up with Savannah.

Due to the boys' mistake, neither Candace nor Savannah had to walk with their exes at the end. Every time Savannah thought of it, she wanted to giggle.

Savannah couldn't see Luke. He sat at the far end of the aisle behind her, which was too much of a turn for Savannah to attempt while standing up front.

Billy Ray could see him though. Savannah suspected that Luke must have looked at her regularly, based on the occasional scowl that crossed Billy Ray's face.

As Anna and Landon declared their love for each other, Savannah's mind kept drifting back to that moment in the garden. There was no doubt that she felt an attraction for Luke. Who wouldn't? He was thoughtful, kind, helpful, and she couldn't even get started on his looks.

In fact, based on how every single girl was watching him as they dashed to the church, he wouldn't be single for long. Not if they could help it.

Did she have time for this? When would she go out on a date? She had the puppies, the dogs and the cats. And Boone.

The minister pronounced the couple husband and wife, and the organist began playing the recessional. Landon and Anna moved up the aisle, and Savannah and Candace glanced at each other with a grin, waiting for the boys to realize they were out of order.

Frederick and Violet met at the center and proceeded out of the sanctuary.

Billy Ray stepped forward, frowning when he saw Candace there.

"Excuse me," he said, trying to pass her to grab Savannah's arm.

But Candace was having none of that. She slid her arm through Billy Ray's with a stiff smile and said, "Escort me and do not make a fuss."

Jeremy looked completely confused but lined up behind Billy Ray to take Savannah's arm. After a stumbling start, Candace and Billy Ray finally moved forward. Savannah struggled to hold back her laughter. It really was just like Billy Ray not to plan ahead even when something mattered as much to him as walking her down the aisle.

Jeremy and Savannah followed them at the proper distance, and she finally got an opportunity to cast her gaze over to where Luke was sitting.

His eyebrows were lifted, and his pinched lips told her he was also trying not to laugh.

Billy Ray must've noticed, because he turned around to look at Savannah as if to confirm that she and Luke were laughing at him.

Well, they were. Billy Ray slowed down and stumbled in his step, but Candace gripped him more firmly and dragged him out the door.

The wedding party descended the stairs to the bottom level so that the guests could filter out. They would return for pictures once the sanctuary was clear.

Anna positively glowed. She couldn't take her eyes off her finger, which now sported a wedding band in addition to her engagement ring.

"We did it! We did it!" she kept saying over and over. She hugged everybody, and Billy Ray had the good sense not to complain about the order of the recessional and put a damper on her excitement.

The photographer hurried into the room. "I'm going to steal the bride and groom for some shots in the gardens," he said. "We'll all meet up by the altar in ten minutes."

"I'm going to go find Luke," Savannah said.

Violet sidled up close to her. "I saw you two getting cozy in the garden," she said. "I was a little surprised that he was bringing you, but now I see it."

Savannah glanced nervously over at Billy Ray. "I'll see you guys when we do pictures."

She raced swiftly up the stairs before Billy Ray could say anything or catch her arm.

Luke had already been enlisted to help Felicia pack up the gifts. When Savannah approached, Felicia said, "I don't know what I would've done without this young man today. It's always so much harder when the wedding isn't in Applebottom proper. We lose half our help."

Luke grinned at Savannah. "I'll just run this out to her car, and then I'll be all yours."

Felicia's grin got even bigger at that. "Oh, I do love love," she said. "Weddings are the best places to find all the young romance."

Savannah's heart beat a little faster. What was everybody seeing? What would make Felicia talk about love? And make Billy Ray so angry? She decided not to wait inside while Luke carried the box. She didn't want Billy Ray to find her alone.

Felicia prattled on about how beautiful the day was, and it didn't get any prettier than this for a wedding in Missouri. Luke loaded the box into her trunk and Felicia kissed his cheek, saying not to worry about her, but she would get more help on the other side.

Savannah and Luke paused on the sidewalk, looking toward the garden, where the photographer posed the happy couple in a kiss, Anna's long veil floating in the breeze.

"She seems really happy," Savannah said.

"They both do," Luke agreed. Their hands brushed against each other as they walked, and Savannah's cheeks burned. Why did it seem so natural that they would hold hands? She stepped just a little farther away to avoid the complication of them deciding or not deciding to close their grip like he had in the garden. She still feared Billy Ray making a scene.

When they got back inside the church, the family had gathered to wait. Luke and Savannah sat in a pew.

Anna's mother approached. "Thank you so much for being one of Anna's bridesmaids. It's so important to her." Her gaze fell on Luke. "I don't think I've met your young man."

More assumptions. "This is Luke. He's Mayor T-bone's son."

Anna's mother turned to her in confusion. "The Mayor has a son?"

Luke himself extended a hand. "I'm Luke Southard. My arrival in Applebottom was a surprise to everyone, including T-bone."

Anna's mother folded a cloth handkerchief on her lap. "I guess I've been so distracted by the wedding that I hadn't even heard. It's very nice to meet you. I'm sure T-bone was delighted."

"Well he was surprised, that was for sure."

Thankfully, they didn't need to go any deeper into the story, because the happy couple returned with the photographer.

After a round of hugs, and Violet fixing Anna's hair and makeup, they ran through a full complement of photographs. When they were done, Anna asked, "Does everyone have a ride over to the reception? We can squeeze a few people into the limo with us."

Violet and Candace opted to ride with the couple, since their families had already headed across town. But Savannah went with Luke.

"You knew you were in it for the day, I hope," Savannah said as they sat at a red light.

"It's been fun."

"Hauling boxes and holding flowers?"

"Seeing you with your friends. And you don't even have one mud smear on you."

Savannah shook her head. "How will I ever resist that sweet talk?"

They grinned at each other like giddy kids.

The hall was decent sized, filled with long tables

decorated with peach table cloths. A DJ had set up in one corner, even though he wasn't playing yet. White lights were strung all across the ceiling, giving the room a fairy-like glow.

Luke drifted into the crowd as Savannah stood with the rest of the wedding party to greet guests. Billy Ray pushed his way beside her. "Pretty crummy when your best girl won't even walk up the aisle with you like she's supposed to."

"You guys were in the wrong order. That wasn't our fault," Savannah said.

Savannah waited out the hugs and handshakes as the guests greeted the couple, then she fell back into the crowd. This was the part she had dreaded, when she would be forced to sit next to Billy Ray in front of everyone, and Luke would be alone among the guest tables taking Boone's spot.

But one thing she hadn't counted on was Felicia. When she arrived at her assigned chair at the long table for the bridal party, she realized that Violet was placed on one side of her and a hastily made card that read *Luke* was on the other.

Candace passed behind her. "Interesting," she said. "Billy Ray is way over there by me."

"Where's Jeremy?" Violet asked.

They walked along the table. Jeremy was seated on the other side of Frederick, who was by the groom. Somehow, none of the exes were near each other.

"Works for me," Candace said, sliding in her chair.

"You won't hear me asking questions," Savannah said. She looked out over the crowd to spot Luke wandering the tables. She waved him over. "Felicia gave you a spot next to me up front. Is that okay?"

Luke shrugged. "Sounds great. Otherwise, I'd probably spend the reception chatting up elderly ladies."

"Too bad for the ladies," Savannah said. "You are mine."

She slipped her arm through his, her face warming up at what she'd just said. But it seemed right.

Savannah spotted Billy Ray behind the tables, scowling at the cards. He picked up his as if he might move them around.

"Let's sit," Savannah said. "Before Billy manages to undo the order."

But Violet was on it. She took the card from Billy Ray and put it back where he found it. The bride and groom moved to their seats, and the room generally settled down.

Savannah looked out over the guests, and for the very first time, wondered what her own wedding might one day look like. She'd never even considered the thought.

Why was she now?

But when she turned to Luke to catch him watching her with an expression of pure tenderness, *she knew.*

This wedding was pretty typical as far as weddings go. Not that Luke had been to many.

The toasts had just ended, and the DJ was calling the bride and groom down for the first dance.

Savannah leaned in. "Halfway through the song, I will have to dance with one of the groomsmen."

"Not Billy Bob," I hope," he said.

Savannah clapped her hand over her mouth to avoid a loud laugh. "No. Candace and I have an agreement that I'm to grab Jeremy and she will dance with Billy Ray."

"When do I get to dance with you?" Having Savannah in his arms would be plenty payment enough for the work he'd done at the wedding.

"The DJ will make an announcement inviting everyone up. You can cut in then. Jeremy won't care."

The table began to empty as the wedding party moved toward the dance floor. Luke stuck with Savannah, keeping his eye on Billy Ray.

Candace moved into position to snag him, and Savannah stepped close to Jeremy. Watching all this unfold was entertaining, like the wedding party version of musical chairs.

The music began, and the bride and groom walked out to the center of the dance floor. Billy Ray continued to try to edge his way closer to Savannah.

The song was slow and felt like it would never end. But at last, the maid of honor and best man stepped out to join the couple on the dance floor. Billy Ray rushed over to Savannah, but Luke cleanly sidestepped in front of him, giving her time to take Jeremy's arm.

Candace more or less stomped over to Billy Ray and dragged him out into a dance.

A few of the people closest to them tittered lightly.

Luke couldn't help but flash a wicked smile. Candace definitely had Savannah's back.

The DJ invited the mother of the groom and the father of the bride out to have their dances. Billy Ray tried once again to turn loose of Candace and head toward Savannah, but Candace kept a vice grip on his arm. The music switched to a new song, and the DJ invited the guests onto the dance floor.

That was Luke's cue. He swiftly approached Savannah, and Jeremy released her. Before Billy Ray could even get across the room, they were already circling the space.

He scowled at them as they passed.

"And here I thought *Billy Bob* and I were going to be good friends," Luke said.

"Don't call him that to his face or he'll try to hit you again," Savannah said with a laugh.

"Sensitive topic?"

"He hates that name. He says it sounds like a cartoon hillbilly."

"Billy Ray is not much better."

"He was named after the singer."

They moved along the floor, and finally, Luke began to relax. All the tough parts were over.

Savannah hadn't been forced to sit by her ex, or dance with him.

She seemed to realize it too, because her body gradually grew less stiff.

One good thing about weddings was that he could count on them to play slow songs that gave you an excuse to hold somebody close.

"I swear, a wedding is harder than taking care of twenty animals a day," Savannah said.

"I believe it," Luke said. "But now is your time to just be chill."

She let out a long sigh, and he drew her a little closer. He navigated them through the other couples, the music washing over the rumble of the guests who were talking at their tables.

As they grew more familiar with each other's movements, they danced like one person, slipping in and out of the lights, cocooned in the happiness that surrounded them.

Luke had never felt quite this tender toward a woman. But then, he'd never felt quite as settled as he did in Applebottom.

As one song blended into another, he sensed that Savannah didn't want to leave the dance floor. He hoped the slow songs would hold out for a while before the DJ pulled out a rock anthem or the chicken dance. Savannah's body began to melt closer and closer to his, until finally, her head rested on his shoulder.

At that moment, his body flooded with emotion.

This felt exactly right, more right than anything he'd ever known in his twenty-five years.

The song crooned on about one true love. He caught a glimpse of the bride and groom, staring starry-eyed at each other. He knew exactly what they felt. This rightness. This absolute perfection.

He released Savannah's hand and slid a long length of her hair behind her shoulder.

She made no move to pull away, and rested her free hand on his waist. But she did look up.

No words passed between them. They weren't necessary. The disco light overhead flashed its brilliant bits of color over her face. She was the most beautiful thing he had ever seen.

And even though it was risky, and they were in public, and her ex-boyfriend, who'd come swinging at him just a few days before stood nearby, Luke discovered he couldn't stop himself. He lowered his face to the tilt of Savannah's, and brushed his lips against hers.

She didn't pull away. They stopped dancing, although the other guests continued their slow circle.

For them, time had stopped. Something was happening here. Something unexpected. Incomprehensible.

And perfectly right.

CHAPTER 13

Savannah didn't even know what to do with herself on Monday morning as she waited for Luke to arrive at the shelter. All day Sunday she had stopped in front of mirrors and touched her lips, wondering if it was really true that she had kissed the mayor's son at a wedding in front of everybody.

The reception had gone on as usual. Anna and Landon had cut their cake and fed each other. Landon had thrown the garter, and Jeremy, of all people, had caught it.

A general conspiracy was created to make Candace catch the bouquet, but she caught on and stormed to the bathroom until it was over.

Likewise, Savannah made sure she was not in range of catching the flowers. She'd already started enough talk with the kiss. Thankfully, one of the elderly ladies from the church had gone after it, pleasing the crowd.

The rumor mill hadn't moved too quickly, because when Savannah got home, Flo hadn't heard anything yet. The speed with which Applebottom citizens would call and text each other when a juicy tidbit came about was mind-boggling. But they'd gotten a little reprieve.

Luke had kissed her once more, just lightly, when he dropped her at her front door after the wedding.

Savannah didn't know how things would be between them now. Would they kiss a lot? Never again?

Would they go out on an actual date, not a fake one?

Was she going to go crazy before she figured any of this out?

Boone walked into the kitchen and sat at the table. He didn't seem to remember any of the conversation with Luke and Savannah from two nights before, or his confusion about who was getting married.

"Eggs okay for breakfast?" she asked.

"Are they fresh? You've been getting store-bought lately."

Savannah whirled about. His voice sounded like normal Boone. Like this was one of the best days, the days where he was almost his old self. They were so rare.

She spoke carefully. "Mrs. Hutchins brought them by yesterday as thanks for protecting her chickens. She also wanted to see the Doberman we took in over it. I don't think she's mad anymore."

"Sounds good then," he said. "How many of her chickens did you say he got?"

Wow. A normal conversation. Tears sprang to Savannah's eyes. She took the eggs out of the refrigerator as if nothing were different. She didn't want to jinx it.

"Five or six. Which is a lot for her."

"She always liked her chickens. How are her grandkids? Didn't they just have another great-grandbaby?"

"Almost. Mandy is due at Thanksgiving."

"That'll be nice." Boone looked around as if he were coming out of a long sleep and just now recognizing where he was. "Should I go check on the dogs? Have they had their morning feed?"

Now a small panic zipped through her. If he wanted to do too much, and he went back into his fog in the middle, she could have a situation on her hands. She needed to keep him right here.

"We can do it together when I'm done. Would you fetch some plates and juice glasses?"

To her relief, he got up and headed to the proper cabinet. He really was having a good day. While he fetched the dishes, she quickly put some bacon on to fry. She wanted to ask him a thousand questions. She had a list upstairs titled *things to ask Boone when he's having a good day*, but she didn't dare run up and get it at the moment.

She tried to think quickly about what was on it. And how to phrase it so that she didn't tip him off that he didn't normally have the answers.

"Boone, do you remember where the charter for the

shelter is? It wasn't with the house title in the safe when I checked."

"David Livingston has it in his files."

Small slip there, but that was okay. Micah Livingston had taken over his father David's practice three years ago. Boone could have easily forgotten that detail.

Still, if they had the charter in their office, she could get it from Micah.

"I'm sure he stuck it somewhere," she said carefully. "And one time you told me about some little life insurance policy you took out on me when I was a baby. I never have found any records of that."

"Now that would be in a box of your mother's things," he said. "She's the one who insisted." His face twisted in sorrow as he set the plates on the table, almost as if he'd forgotten about that loss until this moment.

Oh. She could see him slipping away, his back hunching over, his hands fumbling. He didn't bother to move the juice glasses from the counter to the table, but sat down in his chair. "Are you making flapjacks?"

Tears sprang in Savannah's eyes for real then, and she wiped them away quickly. "We were planning on eggs, Boone," she said. "Are you hungry enough for eggs and flapjacks both?"

Boone looked out the window. "Eggs are okay, I guess. Are they fresh?"

"Really fresh. Mrs. Hutchins brought them over from her coop."

"Mrs. Hutchins? I thought she moved to Springfield."

He was definitely lost. He was thinking of the first Mrs. Hutchins, the current Mrs. Hutchins's mother-in-law. But there was no point in correcting him. "She was visiting."

Savannah wondered if talking about her mother had sent him back. Anything could. Or it was nothing. Just the whims of the severed connections in his mind. The lucid moments were so brief, and she cherished every one.

And she had gotten two very valuable pieces of information this time, the location of the charter and possibly where another document had been put away.

She flipped the bacon and turned the eggs.

Boone stayed quiet while she finished cooking and set the plate on the table. He stared down at the eggs and strips of bacon. "I thought we were having flap-jacks," he said.

"We'll do them tomorrow," Savannah said. He didn't seem agitated, so it should be safe enough to stick with the breakfast she'd already made.

And it was. Boone ate without complaint.

Savannah had planned to bring up the wedding so that she could correct any misperceptions Boone might have, but his sad contemplative expression as he stared out the window kept her quiet. She'd let it go.

It's not like it mattered. If he mentioned it to

anybody else, they would know that she wasn't married to the mayor's son. The confusion wouldn't go past Boone.

The roar of a truck let her know that Luke had arrived. The back door was probably still locked. Savannah shoved down a couple more bites. "I'm going to let the volunteer in, and then I'll be right back," she said.

Boone didn't respond but picked up his bacon. "I like it crisp," he said.

Savannah hurried into the kennel room, sending all the dogs barking. She unlatched each cage and unlocked the back door. The dogs raced into the big yard.

When they were all clear, she headed to the Doberman, now named Nero, and leashed him up.

As she was preparing to take Nero to the smaller yard, Luke came into the room, Luigi at his feet.

"I'll take him," Luke said. "I assume nobody's been fed yet?"

"Not yet," she said. "And, good morning."

"Sorry," he said. "Good morning, Savannah."

They stood there, just looking at each other, until Luigi tugged on the leash to go out with his friends. Luke released his harness and he took off.

"I can take Nero out," he said.

"Okay." She passed him the Doberman's leash.

So that had felt awkward. What did it mean?

Savannah checked on the puppies, who were moving around in their little bay. Tom stretched out his newly freed leg. He wasn't limping, and Savannah knew he was completely on the mend.

"Almost time to move you guys to the kennels," she said. She probably could have already done it, but she liked having them in their special spot. She wished they would be babies forever, but soon she'd have to adopt them out.

Luke came back in. "Brisk out there this morning," he said, rubbing his hands together.

"I thought it might be. The house was sort of cold."

She turned away from the puppies, and this time her breath caught at how Luke was looking at her. Okay, so he definitely hadn't changed since Saturday.

She wanted to ask *so what we do now?* But she couldn't make her voice work.

"So," Luke began, then trailed off.

"I know," she said.

Luke reached out and lightly grasped her hand. "This feels different, doesn't it?"

"A little."

"Are we okay? I mean, I still love coming out here and volunteering. I don't see how any of that should change."

Savannah certainly hoped not. If the cost of the kiss was to lose Luke's help, that was a big price.

But maybe it was worth it. She hadn't felt so hopeful in a long time. So *normal*, like a regular girl finding a regular guy.

"I guess we can treat the daytime as work hours, like

there's a boss looking over our shoulders and we can't get away with anything."

"I can live with that," he said.

"I really need to go finish up with Boone. If you could bring in a bag of feed, I'd appreciate it."

"Anything for you." He lifted the hand he still held and brushed her knuckles across his lips.

Oh, man. Despite what she had *just said* about work hours, it was really obvious that things were going to be very different around the animal shelter.

Luke walked the Doberman around the small yard, practicing basic commands to see if he could get a handle on the dog. They needed to get him in adoptable shape, and he was still pretty wild.

As he circled the yard with the dog, he kept watching for Savannah. They were both trying to act as normal as possible, but it wasn't working. Every time they got within ten feet of each other, Luke wanted nothing more than to draw her into his arms. The fact that they were alone almost all the time didn't help matters. Volunteering at the shelter had become the sweetest form of torture.

At the end of the day, he called in the dogs to give them their final feed. Savannah hadn't asked him to dinner that night, and he didn't want to assume. Truth be told, he didn't know how to behave about anything.

Boone hadn't eaten lunch with them, preferring to watch one of his television programs. Luke assumed he was no longer under the impression that he and Savannah were married. At least he hoped not. Even though he knew that Savannah's father had dementia, and Boone's understanding of the world went in and out, Luke didn't like fooling the old man, even for a moment.

He had just filled the final bowl when Savannah returned from her litter duty in the cat room. "Are you staying for dinner?" she asked.

Luke stood, trying to read the right answer in Savannah's expression. She was maddeningly neutral.

"Should I? How's Boone?"

"Oh, the usual. He had a good moment this morning, but then he lost it. I need to go to the grocery store, but I'm sure I can put together something. There's always sandwiches."

Luke would eat rocks if that meant he got to spend more time with Savannah. "Can I help? I could run into town and pick something up. Maybe I could grab a pizza."

"Pizza!" Savannah said. "I don't remember the last time I got a pizza. No one will deliver way out here and I can't easily run into town to grab one."

"Then it's settled. I'll call it in and then run out and fetch it."

Luke sent a message to T-bone saying he would be out at the shelter for dinner and sailed into town.

Applebottom didn't have any major pizza chains, but Louisa James made pizza out of her house, and anybody in Applebottom knew that you could call her and order one between the hours of five and nine.

He rolled up to Louisa's house and gave two beeps of his horn, like she asked people to do.

Louisa stepped out with a large box. Her riotous black hair flew every direction, and she held it down with one hand.

"T-bone normally orders something with more meat," Louisa said, passing the box and accepting his cash.

"This one's all mine," he said.

"Funny," Louisa said. "It's a lot of pizza for one man."

She was trying to wheedle a little information out of him, like most of the people of Applebottom. Louisa was funny, though, tenacious and energetic. He knew that she had cared for her mother in the little house on the south side of town for years. Some folks worried that life was passing her by. She'd just turned forty, which he only knew because he'd been at Annabelle's Café with T-bone when they brought out a slice of pie with a candle and sang.

She'd been sitting by herself, although the whole restaurant had joined in and once everyone figured it out, she'd had plenty of company.

Probably gossip was one of the only ways she really got to know what was going on. In a lot of ways, her situation was much like Savannah's.

"I worked up an appetite," Luke said. "Thank you."

"You're welcome," she said. "Tell Savannah I said hello and that two pieces have tomatoes cut the way Boone likes."

Luke shook his head as he headed to the shelter. Gossip by pizza toppings. Only in Applebottom.

By the time Luke made it back to the shelter, Boone was sitting at the table, and Savannah had lit the candles again. It had become a little joke between them, how to turn any night into something fancy. She'd conjured up some salad go with it, and already had a fresh pitcher of sweet tea. That girl was a wonder.

Savannah doled out slices, and they ate in silence. Luke had been a hard worker most of his life, and certainly, nothing tasted better than a meal after a long day's haul.

Boone kept his eye on both of them as he chewed his pizza. Finally, he said, "So did y'all already do your honeymoon?"

So he did remember. Luke shifted his gaze to Savannah, curious as to what she would say.

"No, Boone." She bit her lip. "Luke and I aren't married. I went to *Anna's* wedding."

Boone nodded for a moment, as if he understood. Then he said, "I didn't get to walk you down the aisle."

Savannah's eyes glistened. "You will when it's time," she said. "I promise."

Boone set down a slice, his eyebrows drawn

together. "I don't understand what's happening. Why am I so confused?"

Savannah got up from her chair and walked around to put her arm around her father. "It's all right, Boone. We're here."

Now it was the old man who had tears dripping from his eyes. "I can't tell you how happy I am that you found a man. I need to know my little girl is taken care of." He petted her head awkwardly, as if she were a small child. Her hair began to fall out of the ponytail, but she still stood there, holding onto Boone.

He looked at Luke. "You have to promise me to take care of my little girl. She's all I've got."

Luke's stomach felt heavy. But he knew the right thing to say. "I will, sir. I will."

Savannah continued to hold onto Boone's shoulders, but he suddenly sat up straight. "Girl, why are you hanging on me? Go over there and finish up. We have work to do after lunch."

His voice was stern, a tone that Luke had never heard.

Savannah immediately stood up and headed over to her chair.

He didn't know how Savannah did this from day to day.

The conversation moved wildly from subject to subject, led by Boone. The price of gas. Episodes of *Gunsmoke*. When to rotate the tires on a Chevy they didn't own anymore.

Eventually, he shuffled to the living room to watch TV, and Savannah braced her elbows on the table, her head in her hands.

"I didn't lie," Luke said. "I will be here."

But when Savannah turned her head to look at him, looking more like a lost child than a young woman, he wondered if even he could be enough.

The next two weeks were as idyllic as Savannah felt her life could be. A couple of dogs came and a couple of others went. The puppies moved into a normal kennel, and Savannah reluctantly added their picture to the online network of animals needing homes.

She and Luke made out, *a lot*. Despite what she had said about work hours being work, literally the minute the last feeding was over and they decided whether Luke would stay for dinner or not, they were locked together around the back corner of the house, in the feed shed, and anywhere else they wouldn't be seen by the occasional volunteers or Boone.

But she should have known these easy days couldn't last. About two weeks after the wedding, Luke had just left to have dinner with T-bone at the RV Park when the dogs went crazy in the backyard. She looked up from where she was working with Nero.

For a moment she thought maybe Luke was coming back, but then she spotted the uniform on the man by the back gate. What was this about?

She hurried toward the fence. It wasn't her friend Jeremy, but Officer Stone.

Officer Stone had the air of a man who always dreaded dealing with the negative side of the world, even though he encountered it often. He'd been an officer for as long as Savannah could remember, although he'd been a deputy like Jeremy up until a few years back.

He was handsome, and some of the middle-aged ladies in Applebottom were known for calling him out whenever they heard the slightest noise just to take a gander at him. Savannah was pretty sure he didn't pay them mind. He seemed too stern to get his head turned.

"Can I help you?" she asked.

Officer Stone aimed his thumb back at the road. "I passed a truck on the way out here. I guess that was Luke Southard?"

"Probably. He just left. He was volunteering, of course. He does every day."

Savannah wasn't sure why she felt the need to emphasize that he'd been out here to help her. But something in Officer Stone's expression filled her with concern.

"Have you seen much of Billy Ray Baxter since he got back in town?"

Savannah's stomach clenched. What was that boy up to now?

"Sure," Savannah said. "We were both in Anna Bond's wedding a few weeks back."

Officer Stone sniffed. "He been out here?"

"A couple times. He let me know he was back in town a month ago. He wanted to escort me to the wedding."

"Did he? Escort you, that is?"

"No." Now she was going to have to bring up that fake date to an officer. "I went with Luke."

"That's what I've been hearing," Officer Stone said. He leaned on the fence. They were still standing on opposite sides. At least the dogs had calmed down, other than Nero, who continued to bark from his small yard.

"Is there a problem?" Savannah asked, although she really wasn't sure she wanted to know.

"Somebody poured paint all over Billy Ray's Camaro," Officer Stone said. "Did a lot of damage."

Oh, no. That was bad.

"And you think Luke might've done it?" Savannah didn't believe it for a minute, but these other people probably didn't know him as well as she did.

"I don't know about that," Officer Stone said. "Generally speaking, when somebody accuses somebody of something in the same breath as saying it happened, there's bound to be more to the story."

"Luke's not really the sort of guy to do something crazy," Savannah said. "He's been volunteering out here for nearly two months."

"He and Billy Ray have any fallouts?"

Savannah remembered the fight that Billy Ray had attempted.

"Billy Ray didn't much like it that I went to the wedding with Luke. But that's Billy Ray's problem, not Luke's."

Officer Stone nodded. "I get your meaning. Seems more like Billy Ray would've done something crazy, not Luke."

"Exactly." Savannah let out a breath. "But I'm sure Luke was heading to the RV Park if you want to catch him there."

Officer Stone stared down at all the dogs. "I've been meaning to fetch me a new dog. Are all these up for grabs?"

"They are. I do have a Doberman that we're training that might be a good fit for you, though."

"Hmmm," he said. "Let me take a look."

The two of them headed back to greet Nero, and Savannah wondered if she should try to warn Luke about the situation before Officer Stone could get out there.

The officer looked over the dog, who thankfully obeyed all the commands Savannah gave him. "I want to think about this one," he said. "You let me know if anybody else comes for him."

"I will," she said.

He gave her a curt smile. "Don't you fret about Luke. I don't buy Billy Ray's story at all. But somebody damaged his car, and I've got to figure out who it was."

"I understand," Savannah said. "Thank you."

When he left, it took everything in Savannah's control not to start yelling at the walls. Billy Ray probably had a thousand people he'd ticked off. Luke had no reason to do anything to that Camaro.

She sent a quick text to Luke to let him know that Officer Stone was headed that way and what happened. Luke thanked her for the heads up, and then went silent, no doubt because Officer Stone had arrived.

Savannah felt sure they would get this straightened out, but there was one thing she knew for sure. Luke was being kind to Applebottom, but Applebottom was not necessarily being kind to him.

Well, this evening was going from bad to worse.

Officer Stone had just left after asking him a bunch of questions about Billy Ray the troublemaker, who was blaming Luke for pouring paint on his Camaro.

The officer hadn't seemed too concerned about it yet, but Luke knew that all it took was them not finding somebody else before they came circling around back to him.

T-bone stood at one of the grills at the RV Park and flipped a steak over, the fat sizzling over the coals.

"Don't tell me you're worked up over Officer Stone coming out here. Nobody thinks you did it."

"No, it's not that."

"Then what else? Everything okay with Savannah?"

"She's all right. It's the vet school."

"They're not going to take you?"

"They will, but not the way I'd like. I stand to lose most everything I've done."

Fisher College said they could only align a paltry semester of the two years he'd finished in Montana with their curriculum, meaning that he was down something like twenty grand in schooling if he stayed here to finish his work.

They suggested that he become a veterinarian tech instead, since they couldn't offer the animal science and vet school combination he'd been in up north. He'd need a four-year degree, and *then* apply to vet school.

He thought about all the blood, sweat, and tears that went into those tuition fees. The hours of volunteering and acquiring experience hours.

Poof. Up in smoke.

He hadn't realized how unusual his old vet school program had been.

No, Applebottom wasn't working out well at all, and Billy Ray was just the bitter icing on a moldy cake.

T-bone forked the steak and slid it onto a plate. "Medium rare. All yours."

Luke stood up from his chair and accepted his dinner.

T-bone dropped a second steak on a plate and settled in his chair. The wooden rocker creaked under his weight, a familiar sound to Luke now. They often had dinner out on the porch of the convenience store.

"You remember that conversation we had back with the town lawyer when you first came?" T-bone asked.

Luke shrugged. "I don't know. Maybe."

"Micah was in a bad place with his girl, Lorelei. And I told him that if he had the chance to make clear how he felt, he should. Because sometimes, time runs out."

Luke set down his fork. "How did you feel about my mother? We never have talked about her."

T-bone stared off at the cold, dark lake.

"I didn't know her very long. Maybe six months. We didn't live here. We were farther south, in Georgia. She was a brooding type, your mom."

"Don't I know it."

"It suited me. I was a little dark myself."

"So why did she leave? She never would tell me, only that she tried to write you letters, but never sent him."

"I think it had to do with you. She was lighter at the end, just before she left. She laughed more. But I didn't change."

T-bone turned the plate around on his lap, as if he

was looking for the best position for his next cut. But he didn't pick up his knife or fork.

"So she left because she was happy?" Luke asked.

"I think maybe, yes. I think it scared her. When you live the life of darkness, you figure out how to cope. It's when the light comes in that you realize how much you have to lose."

He looked over at Luke, and his black eyes glittered from the lights strung around the porch. "I'm not saying our situation is anything like yours. But Savannah has had her head down for two years. She's scarcely been able to see the color of the sky. But you've been a big help to her. And I think maybe she's seen a little bit of what normal life can be. That creates expectations. You could let each other down. That's scary for both of you."

He sawed off a piece of meat. "I think that's probably why that vet school letter is getting to you. You've got some hard decisions. And you know how hard it will be for her if you leave."

T-bone was right. Right now, he could stay there and help her on the small level forever. Or he could take a risk and leave for about two years to finish school and come back with a lot more options for them.

But there were creeps like Billy Ray around, and she might be vulnerable during that time. And Boone could take another turn.

He sure didn't know what to do.

CHAPTER 15

Over the next few days, Savannah's concern about Billy Ray's accusations began to calm. T-bone had vouched for his son's whereabouts, and nobody was going to question the Mayor. Half the town was afraid of him.

For once, Savannah was glad. It was necessary in this case to avoid anybody falling for whatever Billy Ray was up to. He probably poured the paint on the car his own dang self, just to be spiteful.

Luke was definitely more absorbed after that day, though. Savannah worried that he was finding Apple-bottom to be no good.

She had an idea for what she thought might help. She knew Luke was still trying to work out a deal with Fisher College. She didn't have any clout with the school, not anymore, but she knew someone who did.

Luke agreed to hang out at the shelter and pop in on

Boone for an afternoon, so Savannah could go meet with the director of the shelter in Branson about how to better promote the animals they often moved between them.

While she was in town, Savannah would take the opportunity to also make a stop to see a veterinarian who had always been close to her family.

When she popped into the clinic, she didn't recognize the receptionist sitting at the desk. It wasn't surprising, since a couple of years had passed since she last made it there.

"Can I help you?" the woman asked.

"I'm here to see Dr. Brigham."

The woman stood up to look for an animal, and seeing none, asked, "Do you have an appointment?"

"Dr. Brigham is an old friend of my family. He said that this would be a good time to stop by."

"I'll let him know."

Savannah walked around the foyer while she waited. The clinic operated a mini shelter, just a few dogs and cats who lived in a glassed-in area next to the waiting room. With the steady flow of pet lovers coming in and out, the animals here got adopted swiftly. And it was simpler paperwork, since the practice already knew most of the families.

It was a great system, and sometimes when Savannah was overflowing at her shelter, she would take a few of her best candidates to Dr. Brigham's office.

The girl returned. "You can go on back," she said. "Do you know where you're going?"

"I do. Thank you."

Dr. Brigham hadn't changed, his fuzzy white hair and friendly features making him look like a grandfatherly Danny Glover.

"So what brings you here today?" he asked, walking from behind his desk to envelop Savannah in a hug. "You know if you have some animals that need emergency shelter, you can always just call."

"No, it's something a little more involved than that," she said.

They settled in their chairs.

"How is your father?"

"We manage okay," Savannah said. "He doesn't live in this time and place too often anymore, but we find ways to work around it."

"I miss talking to him," he said with a sigh. "We would get in the liveliest debates about the most mundane elements of animal care. For a layperson, he always knew so much about the animals. I think he could set a broken bone better than I could."

"I learned a lot from him. And from you." She shifted on the chair. "I seem to remember that you are on the advisory faculty of Fisher College in the veterinarian school."

"I am. Were you thinking about applying for the vet tech program? I could definitely put in a good word for you. But is that possible? With Boone?"

"It's not about me. I have a volunteer, a really good one. He comes full-time Monday through Friday."

"That's a lot of hours."

"He's very devoted. And he was in a program in Montana where you could combine a Bachelor's in Animal Science with veterinary school. But then he moved down here."

Dr. Brigham nodded with understanding. "I know the one. Fisher College isn't like that. It's traditional. You finish your Bachelor's Degree and then you apply to the veterinary school and complete the studies. Last I checked it was three hundred hours in animal-related work as well."

"I think he's already done that just with me," Savannah said. "Although since my relationship with Fisher has been severed, I'm not even sure they'll accept my worksheets."

"They will. I'll make sure they will." He braced his elbows on his desk. "So what are you asking exactly?"

"I just, I would hate to lose him. And I think he's going to have to move back to Montana to finish since the schools are so different. They're only accepting a semester of his work."

"But won't you lose him when he finished anyway?"

Savannah hesitated. "I don't know. I like to think I wouldn't."

Dr. Brigham sat back in his chair. "I see. So there is a romantic element to this."

"There is. And normally I would march right on

down to Fisher and try to work out something, bringing all the hours that he's done, his credits, and I'd sit there until we worked something out."

"I see the problem. But unfortunately, our hands are going to be tied here. Unless your friend finishes his Bachelor's Degree first and then applies to the school, we're pretty stuck. If he's taking some specialized courses that work in combination, there won't be any equivalent at our school. It's not something we can just make a phone call and fix. It's part of the degree plan."

"So there isn't anything I can do?"

"Well, like you said, we can ensure that the hours that he's working out there applies when he does get into the veterinary school. We can write some letters and make sure that even if it's been a year or two, they will accept them. He won't have to do it again."

"But as far as getting old school credits..." She trailed off.

"I'm afraid we really can't do anything about that. There are only a couple of schools in the country that do what his old one does. Now it's possible that he could bump his timeline a little shorter, and maybe we can come up with some work-study for some of the things that he's doing with you, and I could fudge a few things as an advisor since he'd be so ahead of the others."

"But still, he would have to start over."

Dr. Brigham sighed. "I'm afraid so. If he stays here,

he'll be set back all the expense and the time that he put into his other studies."

"Well, that's terrible," Savannah said. "Although I know you'd help me as much as you could."

"I absolutely would."

A young man leaned in the open doorway. "Doc, we need you back here."

"I'm coming." He stood up. "It was so good to see you again. And let me work on Fisher for more help for you. They have a new volunteer coordinator, and I can almost certainly get you reinstated. The other girl was quite heartless for her position, and I think I can work on this one."

"Thank you. That would be very helpful."

Even with that assurance, Savannah walked out to her car with a heavy heart.

She knew now why Luke had been so serious last week. It wasn't the Billy Ray issue. It was that school. It was his dream. He knew that to stay in Applebottom with her meant giving up all the work he'd done.

And now she knew it too.

But he was loyal. She'd seen that. He wouldn't leave without a strong push from her.

It was pretty clear what she had to do now. She had to let Luke go, and make it convincing, no matter how much it hurt.

Since the wedding and the shift in his relationship with Savannah, Luke had gotten in the habit of coming out to the shelter even on the weekends, at least for a few hours. He usually did this closer to the end of the day, so that he could help with evening chores and then have dinner with Savannah, and sometimes, her father.

This particular Saturday, Savannah had been more distant than usual. He went over everything he'd said to her the day before, and the text messages they sometimes exchanged late at night, wondering if he had done something wrong.

He'd told her about the problems with the veterinary school, of course, and maybe that was on her mind. He tried to play it off and had not mentioned that he was considering going back to Montana. Not that he was hiding it from her, but he wasn't sure he wanted her to worry about it unless it was actually going to be something he decided to do. He wasn't sure it was.

The fact was, he had a home here. And a father. He was building a group of friends, mostly regulars at the RV Park, but a few of the locals who liked to hang out at T-bone's man-made beach. He worked on a couple of cars a week, which provided him a bit of an income and made a contribution to the town.

The only thing that would really make his world better would be at least a little bit of life with Savannah outside the shelter. Because she was so stuck out there, she was unable to engage with the other young people he was starting to meet. He had no idea how to change that, only that she was more important than anything else.

When all the dogs were fed, he headed to the door between the kennel room and the kitchen. He was still a little uncertain about just storming in, so he often stood there and rapped on the doorframe.

Luigi tried to push past his feet.

"No, puppy dog," he said. "You can't go in." He blocked the pug with his boot. Luigi plopped on his belly in protest.

Savannah stood at the kitchen sink, looking pretty upset.

"Are you okay?" he asked.

"I can't do dinner tonight," she said. "I have plans."

This was new. "Is Flo coming out? Or do you need me to stay with Boone?" He hoped she was getting to see Anna, who was back from her honeymoon, or maybe one of the other bridesmaids. It would be good for her.

"No, my plans are here."

He didn't know what to say to that. "Then I guess I should just clear out?"

"Billy Ray is coming," she said. "I asked him to dinner."

Her words hit him like a punch to the gut. He couldn't believe it. What had changed? They were fine Thursday. And Friday morning. Then she'd gone into Branson without him.

Maybe what she'd really done was meet Billy Ray. And they decided to get back together.

"I see," he said, even though he didn't. "Does that mean I shouldn't come around anymore at all? You need the help." It would kill him to be around her, knowing she was with Billy Ray again, but he couldn't leave her to do all this alone.

"I won't need help anymore, not yours," she said, her voice shaky. "You remember the trip I took yesterday?"

"Yeah, you went to Branson to talk with the people at that big shelter."

"Well, I met with a vet who has promised to get me some more volunteers. So I thought maybe, I should let you go. And let you pursue things. Wherever you needed to do that."

Now, wait a minute. Something seemed fishy here. Despite what she had said about Billy Ray, and the fact Luke wasn't invited in the house, he walked into the kitchen. Luigi trotted in behind him, but Luke let it go.

"Have I done something wrong, Savannah? I thought we were okay."

"Well, we're not. I've got to be here and run the shelter. And you see Boone's clearly going downhill. I just, I just need to do this."

Luke braced his arms on the counter, staring down at the toaster. He couldn't meet Savannah's eyes. This was tearing him up inside, and he didn't know what to do about it.

"You would tell me if I did something wrong, right?"

Her voice sounded strained. "I would," she said. "You didn't do anything wrong at all. This is just what needs to happen."

He wasn't going to let this go. Not without a fight. He turned to her and held onto her shoulders.

"Look me in the eye and tell me you'd rather be with Billy Ray than me," he said. "Because I find it hard to believe that, not when you did everything you could to avoid being around him at the wedding. It doesn't make any sense. Did he put you up to this? Does it have to do with his car? Is he blackmailing you somehow?"

She wouldn't meet his gaze, staring down where Luigi sat between them, whining in concern.

"He's not blackmailing me," she said. "I'm mainly seeing him again because I know that's the surest way to get you out of here."

What? Why was she doing this?

Luke tried to pull himself together. He tried to stay calm. But he couldn't. He wouldn't lose her if she wouldn't even say why.

"Look at me, Savannah. You have to tell me what's going on." He gripped her shoulders and pulled her a little closer. "Look at me!"

Luke didn't see Boone until the man had entered the kitchen at full tilt.

"Get your hands off my daughter!" he bellowed.

Before Luke knew what had hit him, Boone's fist smashed into his jaw. Luigi took off for the kennel room with a frightened bark.

Luke let go of Savannah and stumbled back. There was no way he could fight this old man. But Boone was coming at him, swinging again.

"Boone!" Savannah cried. "Stop!"

She tried to grab for him, but he was intent on following Luke as he backed away.

Luke held up his hands. "I'm leaving," he said. "I don't want to cause any trouble."

He kept backing up until he was in the kennel room.

Boone wrapped his arms around his daughter. "Are you okay, baby girl? I'm right here. Dad is right here."

Luigi whined at his feet. Behind him, Sergeant stood on full alert, his ears pricked. He let out one sharp warning bark. Luigi whined again, then closed his teeth on Luke's pant leg to pull him back.

He could still see Savannah and Boone. He was only a few feet out of the kitchen.

"Just go," Savannah said. "Thank you for everything you've done." She led Boone back to the living room.

So this was it. Luke turned away, Luigi on his heels. Sergeant watched him with a tense expression as he passed by and headed out the back door.

All this time out here. Caring about her dogs. About the shelter. About her.

For what?

For nothing.

CHAPTER 16

The next week was a lot harder for Savannah, trying to manage all the chores alone after having Luke's help for so long. But she did it. She had no choice. The animals needed her.

Sergeant picked up on her distress and began following her all over the house. She didn't stop him. He'd been around long enough now that she should treat him like a personal pet.

Delilah emailed to say that a couple had stopped by after seeing the puppies Tom and Jerry on the adoption site, putting in an application, and never hearing back. She thought they were the perfect fit.

Savannah knew she'd dropped the ball on that. Tons of applications had come in, and she had been merciless about who would get the puppies, turning down everyone as not good enough.

But she was going to have to let them go.

Tears dripped down her face as she wrote Delilah back to say okay, she trusted her judgment. When she pushed away the old laptop, Sergeant did a very-un-Sergeant-like thing and laid his long nose in her lap. She petted his head until she felt better.

If all that wasn't enough, Boone stopped talking completely. It was as if overnight, all his words just vanished. The doctors had told her that every person progresses differently, and there would be lots of forward and back motion in his abilities. But when things started to go downhill, it often happened quickly.

Savannah blamed herself. The big upset with Luke must have been part of it. She'd never seen Boone charge somebody like that, much less punch him.

She called his doctor and booked an appointment. She didn't know how she was going to be able to leave the animals for half a day to drive to Branson, but in the end, Flo took off to take him instead. She told Savannah that she didn't need to be worried about this, and that Flo would help out with her brother.

On Wednesday morning of that terrible week, Flo came out to fetch Boone. He brightened considerably as he spotted his sister, and the words *Flo Bo* were the first thing he'd said in days.

Flo looked at Savannah sympathetically as she helped Boone into his shoes. "I heard your feller was headed back to Montana. You doing okay?"

"I'll be all right." Savannah knew that Luke was leaving. She'd asked Candace and Anna to check around town. She needed to know that he was doing what she wanted, the whole reason she'd split with him. To learn that he would finish vet school was both a relief and a cause for despair.

She was pretty sure she'd fallen in love just to let him go.

Flo patted her back. "I ordered pizza from Louisa and Boone's favorite pie from Gertrude. We should be back in town at about one o'clock, but I'll text you if we get off schedule. If you could go pick those things up before we get back, it'll be a nice surprise for Boone. If you can't, we'll do it."

"I can get away for an hour." She'd have to kennel the dogs midday, but it could be done.

The two of them helped Boone out to the car. The shuffle in his step was even worse than usual. His worn loafers dragged in the dirt, kicking up dust. He sat heavily in the seat of Flo's Oldsmobile as if he was finally resting after a marathon, not a short walk from the porch.

When they left, Savannah treated herself to a good hard crying session, something she hadn't been able to do with Boone in the house. It upset him too much if she cried. So she held it all in until now.

Sergeant kept vigil, at one point nudging a pillow off the sofa to push to Savannah where she sat on the floor. She held on to the doggy and just wailed.

Luke was gone. Boone was worse. She had to do everything herself again. Her friends were all moving on with their lives, getting married and having careers or earning college degrees.

She was stuck in this house in the woods with an ever-changing rotation of dogs and cats that would leave her.

The animals. They needed feeding and letting out into the yard. She couldn't just sit there crying all morning.

When all the big dogs were running around, she felt better. Sergeant kept an eye on her as she went about her chores. He really was a good dog.

She put Nero on his leash and walked him among the others. He was doing really well. Officer Stone hadn't called her, but she knew when to nudge. She would send him a message and tell him that it looked like Nero might be ready for adoption, and she bet he'd be a fine dog for an officer.

When the outside dogs seemed settled, she came back for Tom and Jerry. Their listing needed to come down since Delilah had found a good home. They'd be leaving soon.

She opened the kennel, lifting one in each arm to take into the house.

The three of them sat on the living room floor. She was so out of sorts. She couldn't remember feeling this distraught, other than maybe when Boone was first diagnosed. So much had been going on then. Losing the volunteers. His crazy mood swings.

She'd been too little to really remember the death of

her mother. But sometimes when she sat on the living room floor like this, she would look up and swear she could see her mother in her rocking chair. The image must have been imprinted on some part of her brain even though she couldn't bring the memory up by trying.

The puppies crawled up and down her crossed legs as if they were a mountain range. They tumbled together, biting each other on the ears until one of them yelped.

They helped. Savannah felt her grief slip into something more manageable.

Eventually, the puppies got sleepy, and she took them back into their kennel lined with soft towels. She checked on the dogs outside, and then went into the cat room to sit, immediately having her lap filled with Sweetie, the soft Persian, and a pair of identical black kittens about six months old.

This was why she ran the shelter. When everything else seemed to be falling apart, the animals soothed her. Even though Luke was gone, and one day, maybe not too far away, she would lose Boone, there would always be abandoned pets that would need her.

"Thank you, Mama," she whispered into Sweetie's ear. This is what her mother had always known. Everything could fall apart, but as long as you had a purpose, and a way to help, you could get by.

She had to get to chores. She hauled in feed bags, cleaned out litter, the glanced at the clock. Gracious, it was time to run into town. She lured all the dogs inside with bacon treats.

Then she cleaned herself up and ran a brush through her hair, because going into the pie shop meant being judged by Gertrude and Maude. She really didn't want all old ladies on Town Square talking about pathetic little Savannah Perkins all alone out there in the animal shelter, not even keeping herself groomed. Maybe that was pride talking, but she just couldn't help it.

A pretty bell tinkled as she walked into the bakery, and the smell of spices, sugar, and warm fruit made her want to swoon. She was looking forward to this lunch.

Maude stood behind the counter in her spotless white apron, a huge smile lighting up her face. "Well, there you are," Maude said, coming out from behind the counter to envelop Savannah in a cinnamon-scented hug. "I have Boone's pie all ready."

She returned behind the counter and brought out a crisp white box. "Please say you'll stay for a minute and have a slice of pie. I know this cherry one for Boone, but I seem to recall that your favorite is lemon chess with blueberries."

"I still have to pick up a pizza from Louisa."

"Don't you worry about that," Maude said. She called back to the other room. "Gertie! Ring up Louisa and tell her to hold Savannah's pizza for about ten minutes."

"I'm not your secretary!" a voice replied.

Maude waved the comment away. "She'll do it. She just likes to make a fuss." She moved along the counter in smooth, practiced motions, pulling the pie from the case, cutting a perfect slice, and sliding it onto a plate.

Savannah perched on a stool, her belly rumbling. "Maude, you are too good to me."

"We heard about Boone. You'll have to let us know what the doctor says."

Must have been Flo talking. "He said his sister's name today. His first word in days."

"Well, that sounds promising. Maybe it was just a bad spell." Maude placed the plate with the perfect creamy yellow pie dotted with blueberries before Savannah.

Gertrude walked in from the back. She was the opposite of Maude in every way. Big white hair, pale powdered skin, a surly expression, and an apron that looked like it had been through a food fight.

"Louisa is going to hold your pizza," Gertrude said. "I see you got your favorite pie. Good thing we had one today." She looked at Maude pointedly. "I told you we needed a lemon chess today."

"You did, Gertie, you did."

Gertrude leaned her elbow on the counter. "I knew you'd be by. We made that pie just for Boone. Extra cherries. Less sugar."

Something flashed in Gertrude's eyes that looked suspiciously like sadness. Savannah stared down at her pie. Gertrude was known for her no-nonsense, curmudgeonly attitude. But she was one of the town jewels of Applebottom and the pie shop was a central hub of the town.

"We saw T-bone this morning," Maude said gently. "He said Luke sure has been torn up about your split. You want to talk about it?"

Savannah shook her head. She should've known that this pie would come with a price.

"Well, I'll say it if nobody else will," Gertrude said. "You told that poor boy you were getting back with Billy Ray Baxter. But we know for a fact that can't be true, because one Billy Ray has moved to Charleston, and taken his paint-splattered Camaro with him."

Savannah's fork went still. Billy Ray had moved to Charleston? And Luke knew? What did he think of her now then? He knew she was a big ol' liar.

Her voice was raspy when she asked, "Why?"

Gertrude seemed pleased as punch to spill the news. "Seems like he ticked off some thug from Springfield, and that little paint job was his doing. Billy Ray is on the run since the paint was just a warning of more to come." Gertrude's eyes flashed. "I don't see the two of you having much of a long-distance relationship, not with Billy Ray's predilections."

"No, definitely not." Savannah stared at her pie. "I hope Luke doesn't think he did something wrong."

"I'm sure he does. That boy is beating himself up like an old drum," Gertrude said.

"Have a heart, Gertie," Maude said. "I'm sure whatever happened between the two of them is their business."

A tear slipped down Savannah's cheek, and she tried to subtly wipe it away.

"Just a shame, that's all," Gertie said. "It was a good match."

Savannah continued to eat her pie, even though she could scarcely taste it now. It *had* been a good match. But Luke had places to be. And who knows. Maybe when he was done he'd make his way back. His dad did live here, after all.

No doubt she'd still be here with her kennels and cat room, feeding and adopting out the little lost souls of Applebottom.

The door tinkled again. It was Louisa, holding a large pizza box.

"You've ventured out," Maude said.

"The nurse is in with Mom," Louisa said. "I thought I'd drop off the pizza and maybe grab me a slice while I had a few minutes."

"I'm honored," Maude said. "It isn't often we see you about town."

Gertrude fetched a pie from the case. "Your usual, I assume?"

"Yes, if you have it," Louisa said.

"It wouldn't be Applebottom Pie Shoppe without an apple bottom pie." Gertrude set the pie on the counter and examined it for the best place to make the cut.

Louisa looked over at Savannah. "How you holding up with Boone?"

Savannah tried to sit up a little straighter. "All right. We'll see what the doc says today."

"I know exactly where you are. Mom doesn't have bad days, more like bad months." Louisa smiled at Gertrude as the pie plate slid toward her. "This is one of my best things in life these days."

And Louisa did know. Like Savannah, she'd spent years caring for an aging parent. She was quite a bit older than Savannah, though, and had dedicated her life to her family. Savannah mainly knew her by her pizzas, which she sold to make extra money while she cared for her mother. Her father had passed some years ago.

"Gertie's pies could make anyone feel better about life," Maude said, but Gertrude just rolled her eyes.

"Don't flatter, me, Maude. We all know you made both those pies."

"Based on your recipes," Maude said. "And you do *not* know how to take a compliment."

Savannah caught Louisa's gaze and they both smiled. Maude and Gertrude's sniping was legendary in their town.

"Has Luke left yet?" Louisa asked. "I saw him a couple nights ago when he picked up a meat pizza, no extras for you and Boone. He said he was headed to Montana. I take it you two split?"

Her voice was kind, but the question set Savannah into another tailspin.

"I don't think he's gone yet," she said. "But I haven't talked to him since we broke up."

"Such a shame," Louisa said. "He sure had your stars in his eyes."

Had he? Savannah guessed so. Maybe if she were lucky, they wouldn't totally burn out. Or get eclipsed by some other girl back in Montana.

It was a risk she had to take.

"Thank you for bringing me the pizza," Savannah said. "How much do I owe you?"

Louisa waved her away. "Repay me by talking to him one more time before he leaves."

Savannah pulled her slender wallet from her pocket. "I think I better just give you the money."

CHAPTER 17

*L*uke tied down the last corner of the tarp covering the back of his pickup.

T-bone tucked the loose end of the cord underneath the canvas. "Looks to be about it," he said. "You sure about this?"

"I am," Luke said. "It was a good spell down here. And I'll be back to visit." He nudged T-bone with his elbow. "And you could always head up north, check out the landscape there."

"Maybe so," T-bone said, clapping Luke on the shoulder.

Luke thought he caught a glimmer in the tough man's eye. Dang, this was harder than he expected.

Jeremy took a step toward him and extended his hand for a shake. "It's been good knowing you while you were here, Luke," he said.

"It was nice making some friends. And you don't give up on Candace. She'll come around."

Jeremy let out a little laugh. "If she ever gives me the time of day again, then we'll talk."

"Have some faith. The ones that fight back are often the ones who have the most at stake."

Jeremy's eyebrows lifted. "I think I should tell you to follow your own advice."

He had him there, but there was nothing to be done now. Luke had texted Savannah a couple of times, checking if she could use his help. But she just gave short one-word answers and left it.

Luke whistled for Luigi, who trotted up and jumped into the passenger seat of the open truck. At least that was one little part of Savannah he got to take with him.

He gave everyone a final wave and climbed up into the cab of the truck. The gravel crunched beneath his tires as he drove to the road past the convenience store.

He'd be back. He had to be. He had a dad now. Friends to come back to. And who knew. Maybe in two years, Savannah would have figured things out.

As the pine trees whizzed past him, and he approached the bridge over the lake, Luke thought about that whopper of a lie she had told him about Billy Ray.

He believed her at first, of course. Why wouldn't he? Only later had he found out that Billy Ray wasn't even in town anymore. He'd turned tail and run over whatever lowlife had poured paint on his Camaro.

What he couldn't figure out was why Savannah had done it. She said herself that she was telling him about Billy Ray because it was the surest way to make him leave. Why did he have to leave?

It didn't matter. He was back on track for school with only a semester delay. She'd made her decision. He'd made his. All that was left now was seeing it through.

The drive to Montana would take a good twenty hours. As he approached the Missouri state line, he realized he really did want to get out of the state as fast as possible. Missouri had broken his heart. Even if it had given him a family.

What he needed was to see the state in his rearview mirror.

Luigi started to whine and dance in his seat. Luke rolled his eyes and said, "Already? We're never going to get there."

He spotted a large corrugated metal building as the only break in the landscape. He pulled into their parking lot to find a quiet spot for the dog to relieve himself.

As he got out, he realized that this was a plant nursery. *Missouri Blooms*, a sign said.

Luke put a leash on Luigi. They found a nice bush on the roadside, and Luigi made quick work of his business.

As they walked back toward the truck, they faced a

large marquee, the sort where you use individual letters to form whatever message you had to say.

Today it read, *Last chance to plant spring bulbs before the first freeze.*

Luke should've gotten in his truck. He should've opened the door and loaded up his dog and hightailed it over the state line that was only a few miles away.

But he didn't. He shortened the leash up and headed toward the nursery. Giant walls of mulch and dirt were piled outside the building. People milled through rows of container plants, small trees, and bushes.

A young man, barely seventeen, in a *Missouri Blooms* T-shirt approached. "Can I help you find something, sir?"

"Tell me about the bulbs that you need to plant now to bloom in the spring."

"Well, you got your crocus, and your tulips, lilies, and anemones," he said. "They're predicting the first freeze in about four days. Once the ground is frozen, the bulbs won't make it. You've got to do it now."

"Did you say anemones?" Luke flashed with the memory of Savannah standing in front of the planter of flowers at Anna's wedding, saying anemones were her favorite.

"I did. You can get a mix of colors, or all red, white, or purple."

"And these plants will come up all on their own in the spring?"

The teen led him over to a wall lined with hooks,

each of them sporting little mesh bags holding differ-ent-sized bulbs.

"You can't go wrong with this type of anemone," he said pulling a bag down. "If you wanted a sure thing, I would plant a good amount of these, in a big cluster so it'll really show up. Then I would take some of these others." He pulled two or three bags off their hooks. "These I would mix up a little bit, that way if some come up and some don't, you don't have a big empty hole. That'll be mighty pretty come mid-March."

March. That seemed so far away. But what was he thinking, buying bulbs? He wasn't going to be in Missouri. Not now, not in the spring, and certainly not four days from now when the first freeze hit.

Despite all that, he said, "I'll take them all."

"Very good. Do you need mulch? Fertilizer? Bone meal is good to mix in the soil."

"I'll take whatever I need to make sure they'll sprout up pretty come March," he said.

"I'll put everything together for you on a cart." He pulled several tags off bulb sacks, and the stickers off several other jugs and bags and handed them to Luke. "You can take these up to the cashier and pay and then bring your car around to the loading zone."

Luke headed to the register, Luigi trotting obedi-ently beside him. As he got his truck and backed it up to where the boy was waiting with the cart, his mind raced.

What now? Leave the flowers and supplies for her?

No, he couldn't do that. Savannah didn't have time to plant flowers.

He'd have to plant them himself.

Then what? Sneak away?

As he and the boy rearranged the back of his truck to fit in his purchases, he realized the whole thing was crazy. And pointless. Savannah had pushed him away.

When he pulled out on the highway, he headed for the Missouri state line once more. He would just forget it. He could donate the stuff he'd bought somewhere along the way. What a ridiculous impulse he'd just had.

But as he got closer and closer to the edge of the state, he felt more and more sure he was doing the wrong thing. His head began to clang with alarm.

Leaving was wrong.

Yes, he was going to lose twenty grand in tuition and a couple years of his life in a program that couldn't be transferred anywhere else.

But that was just school. Just classes. In all his days, he'd never met anyone like Savannah. No one as devoted. As kind. As hard-working.

That was the thing that couldn't be replaced. Not the school hours. Not the money or the time.

But her.

Right as they headed toward the sign that read *Leaving Missouri,* he slammed on his brakes and did a crazy U-turn to head back the other direction.

"Were headed home, Luigi," he said. "I'm going to call that college and figure out how to start over. Then we're gonna plants some flowers. You want to see Savannah? Yes? Yes?"

Luigi gave a happy bark and rolled on his back. Luke reached over to scratch his belly. "Exactly, puppy dog. We both know what we want."

CHAPTER 18

Savannah woke up the next day to a crying jag hangover. Luke was gone. She knew this. Jeremy had told Anna, who called her. His truck had left midafternoon yesterday.

The tears had been a lot. Way too much. She had to pull herself together. Self-pity wasn't going to get the dogs fed or the kitty litter cleaned. She threw her covers aside and forced herself to start her day.

At least Boone was all right. His potassium and sodium levels had both been low. That's all. He'd gotten an injection, and now she had a diet and some supplements that would help.

When she entered the kitchen, she saw Boone had gotten up before her and dressed himself in the old farm clothes. She was getting used to this version of her father, the one who dressed and talked like her Grandpop.

It was comforting in some ways. Savannah had only known Grandpop ten years before he had passed on. When Boone got like this, it was sort of like seeing Grandpop all over again.

Luke always told her that she could find the bright side of anything.

But she couldn't find the bright side of him leaving.

No, that wasn't true

The bright side was that Luke would get to finish school. He'd become a veterinarian. Live his dream.

She was living her mother's dream. That was something.

And it wasn't like she would never see Luke again, or hear anything about him. His father was here. And T-bone was part of the Town Square proprietors. They all gossiped something fierce. She would hear about him, at least secondhand.

This was just the way it had to be.

She fixed Boone his breakfast, and not feeling like eating herself, headed to the kennel room to release the dogs into the yard. Today she took out Nero and held onto his collar as they stood by the door.

"Are you up with hanging with the pack today?" she asked him.

She had done lots of test runs with Nero and the rest of the gang under her close supervision. After a few altercations that Sergeant had managed to shut down, Nero finally recognized the German Shepherd as the alpha, and more or less folded in with the pack.

She opened the door and let the big Doberman run with the others.

The whole lot of them had made a beeline for the back fence. That was odd. Was something back there? Probably it was a rabbit.

Although it was getting cold for rabbits. The first freeze was expected any day now, with a cold front blowing down from the north.

"Sergeant?" she called. "Nero! Pudge!"

None of them listened to her at all. She walked out into the yard to see what the fuss was about.

The dogs were all lined up along the fence, sniffing at its edge.

As Savannah approached, she caught the scent of freshly tilled earth and cedar mulch.

That was weird. She didn't have a neighbor close enough for her to be able to smell their gardening.

Only when she got within a few feet of the fence did she realize that a large area on the other side had been landscaped.

What in the world?

She squeezed alongside the dogs. In an area about ten feet long and three feet deep, a fresh layer of mulch was spread. Several little stakes, fashioned from what looked like wire clothes hangers and the label from a plant bag, were set at intervals. Savannah leaned over the fence and peered at them. Crocus. Tulips. Lilies.

Anemones.

Savannah caught her breath. Her favorite.

The dogs quieted down, realizing that the new smells did not pose any threat or even an interesting find. As they began milling the yard again, Savannah passed through the gate to walk around the other side of the fence for a closer look.

She knelt down by the garden, touching the fresh mulch her with her hands.

Who would have done this for her?

She looked around at the woods, and her yard, then turned to peer at the side of the house.

She got so surprised at what she saw that she fell back on her bottom.

Luke's truck was parked out near the road.

She got up and dusted off her jeans, planning to head toward it, when a stout little figure began bounding toward her at top speed.

Well, top speed for an overweight pug.

She knelt down to greet Luigi, laughing when he instantly flopped on his back for a belly rub. "What are you doing here?"

A million thoughts ran through her head. Maybe the dog had been too much trouble on the trip, so Luke had brought him back. Maybe the flowers were his way of saying he was sorry to have to return the dog.

When she looked up, Luke was walking toward her.

Her breath caught. It seemed like forever since she had seen that lanky stride, the tilt to his head, his broad shoulders.

Luke bent down to scratch Luigi behind the ears.

"The bulbs should come up in the spring," he said.

So it *was* him.

"Thank you for planting them," she said. "I never would have made the time."

"You found any volunteers yet?"

So this was how it would be. Small talk. Savannah swallowed her disappointment. "I have somebody coming out a few times a week starting Monday."

"That's good."

"Dr. Brigham, a vet who is good friends with Boone, is going to have the new volunteer coordinator at Fisher College send me more. He feels like enough people have come and gone over there that we can try again. I won't be caught by surprise now. Boone is diagnosed, and I know what I'm dealing with."

His brows drew together. "Is that the same Dr. Brigham who is the advisor of the veterinary school?"

"It is. You know him?"

"I talked to him yesterday."

Savannah's heart sped up. Dr. Brigham followed up on their conversation? She thought they were done. Nothing he could do. That's what he had said. "When?"

"When I got back. I only drove maybe an hour." He laughed. "I saw the flowering bulbs and stopped. When I got back, I called the school and they had a note on file that I should talk to Dr. Brigham."

Savannah's heart hammered painfully. "What did he tell you?"

"He suggested that I get my vet tech license at Fisher.

It would only take a semester to finish with all the things I had already done in Montana plus my hours with you." Luke looked down at the dog, as if meeting her gaze was a struggle right now.

"But you want to be a veterinarian. You were in that program!"

"Dr. Brigham said that if I did a good job and got to know some professors, they could probably work out an arrangement where I'd finish my bachelor's degree, and when I did get to the vet school, I would have a lot of credit. He'd make sure my vet tech work counted for something."

"But won't you still lose everything you did in Montana?"

"More or less, but it's a really good deal. Instead of spending another twenty grand up there trying to finish on the old timeline, I would basically be working my way through here without incurring any more debt. They have a special program for vet school if you're already working in the field. In the long run, it's a better plan."

"Where would you get that extra vet tech work?"

"Right here. Dr. Brigham said between him and Dr. Black, they could be the sponsoring vets for a weekly clinic here at the shelter. I will be the tech." This time he did finally look at her. "I mean, as long as you'll have me." He gave her a grin that melted her bones. "Somebody's got to tend those flowers in the spring. And we know you don't have time."

It took a moment for it all to sink in. And when it did, Savannah lunged forward, surprising both herself and Luke so completely, that she knocked him over, and they landed in the damp dirt.

"You're not leaving?" she asked.

He laughed. "And you're not back with Billy *Bob?*"

She grabbed a smear of mud and rubbed it on his nose. "Of course not."

He touched her cheek, leaving a smudge of wet dirt. "Why are you always so dirty?"

"Oh!" Savannah ran her hands through a good bit of earth, this time smearing his jaw. "Now who's covered in mud?"

Luke laughed and rolled over, smashing her into the dirt. "I like you messy. It means you're a real girl who does real work."

"I'm glad you don't want me to be all fancy."

"I wouldn't know what to do with fancy."

She grabbed his head and made him kiss her, dirt and all. The chilly mud seeped into her clothes, and a pudgy pug sniffed in annoyance that he wasn't being scratched.

And it was absolutely perfect.

CHAPTER 19

Savannah pulled down the wicker picnic basket that she and Boone used every year. She opened the lid, letting her fingers glide across the cups and plates and napkins they only used for this one annual picnic.

She shifted things aside to make room for sand-wiches, chips, some water bottles, and the traditional bottle of orange soda. Neither Boone nor Savannah really liked orange soda, but on this one day, they always drank some.

Even if Boone didn't remember, she'd keep the tradition.

She hefted the basket on her shoulder and headed to the living room. "Five minutes Boone," she said to her father, who was watching *Wheel of Fortune*.

He nodded at her and she checked the clock. She had timed their departure with the end of the show to avoid any hiccups in their leaving. On this day above all others, a fight with Boone would be hard.

She hurried back to the kennel room, where Gayle and her newest volunteer, Gabe, were handling a huge litter of newborn kittens. Savannah was so grateful for the new recruits Fisher College had sent her, because that many kittens, six in all, would have meant she would not have been able to leave the house.

Or else, she wouldn't have taken the kittens in the first place.

It was nice having them. Since Tom and Jerry left last fall, she'd tried to always keep some babies in the sick bay. It helped.

She peeked in at the kittens. "How are they doing?"

Gabe looked up at her, his merry eyes bright and happy. He sure did love the animals. He was going to be a great vet one day. "Jasmine and Aurora are eating well, and Belle is starting to get the hang of the bottle. Moana is greedy and keeps trying to eat Elsa's breakfast. And Tiana was a little sluggish today. I'm keeping an eye on her."

"Who would've thought all six kittens would be girls," Savannah said, reaching out to stroke their fuzzy little heads.

Gayle looked up from where she was filling one of the tiny eyedroppers. The kittens were only three weeks old. "And who would've thought Mr. Brown Eyes here would've named them all after Disney princesses."

Gabe shrugged. "I have three little sisters. It's all I know."

"Well, it looks like you have it under control," Savannah said. "I should be back in a couple hours. At least one of you can stay that long?"

"I'll be here," Gabe said. "I need more experience with newborn cats anyway."

"I'll be sure to make a note in your file about your hours with them," Savannah said.

She patted her leg two times, and Sergeant popped up from his bed in the corner. Savannah gave him regular breaks from his duties as the chief of the yard dogs. Sergeant needed a little time to just be an ordinary pet. The two of them returned to the living room.

Boone perked up when he saw the dog. "Come here, Sergeant," he said. He looked over at Savannah. "Is he coming with us?"

"I thought it would be fun."

Savannah picked up the basket and the three of them headed out to Boone's truck. Late February was still pretty cold, and Savannah bundled her jacket more tightly around her as she helped Boone into his side of the truck.

As they drove along the highway, the familiar melancholy settled over her. She didn't mind it. The feeling connected her to her mom. She was so little when her mother had died that she didn't have a lot of solid memories to attach to her. But this aching pressure in her chest was something she could always count on to help her get in the right mindset for this day.

For the very first time, she and Boone wouldn't be doing this alone. As they pulled into the cemetery, she spotted Luke's truck already parked along the road that wound its way through the headstones.

Savannah had given him a rough location of her mother's grave. It was nice that he had gone there ahead of them, so they didn't have to wait. She glanced over at Boone. Last year, the picnic had been cut pretty short because he didn't know why they were there and didn't want to stay. Today, though, he scratched his stubbly chin and looked out thoughtfully over the cemetery, as if he might be conjuring old memories.

This definitely wasn't easy, whether Boone remembered or not. She was glad for Luke, someone to walk this path with her.

As she parked, she spotted him sitting on a bench near where she told him to be. He looked strong and masculine in a camel coat and a ball cap from the RV Park. He walked up to the truck and opened Boone's door.

"I have a basket in the back," she said.

He nodded, his face solemn. Savannah walked Boone out among the headstones until they reached her mother's. They stood there a moment, looking at the grave.

Savannah wasn't sure Boone knew what was going

on, but then he said, "So many years gone. You were such a small thing. Still feels like yesterday."

Savannah's eyes smarted, grateful that Boone was aware of where they were and why they had come. Luke hung back near the truck, holding the picnic basket and blanket. Savannah turned and waved him forward.

"He knows," Savannah whispered as she showed Luke where to spread the blanket.

"That's good, right?"

"Yes, it is."

Boone turned to them. He looked at Luke a little curiously for a moment, then said, "It's nice for you to come out here."

"Happy to," Luke said.

Savannah sat next to the basket and began to unload. Whenever Luke was around, they never knew if Boone would remember exactly who he was. He did seem to recognize that Luke helped out at the shelter. And he never acted antagonistic, as if he didn't remember punching him once.

She and Luke were slowly figuring out the details of how to set up the clinic. Luke would be finished with his vet tech certification by June, and they needed to have a place for him ready.

T-bone had volunteered to assemble a prefab outbuilding for them to use, and it was supposed to be delivered during spring break, when Luke would have the week off and could put it together.

It would be nice to have another space, if for nothing

else than to spread out her volunteers instead of crowding everyone in the cat room and the kennels.

Boone sat down with them, and Savannah passed him a sandwich and spread some chips on his plate. Luke helped sort the food out, pausing when he got to the bottle of orange soda.

"That was mom's favorite," Savannah said. "Boone and I always split a bottle in her honor when we come out here."

"I've never seen you drink it."

She laughed. "Boone and I can't stand it. We do it for her."

A cold wind whipped at her hair, and she zipped her jacket all the way to her neck.

"Was it this cold on that day?" Luke asked.

"An ice storm," Boone said. "Lena had pulled over because she saw an injured dog on the side of the road." He picked up a chip, then set it down again. "The couple was driving back from some sort of party. He saw her car and swerved to avoid it, then overcorrected on the other side. He never saw her or the dog. Got 'em both."

Savannah guessed that some details could be so buried in your mind, making so many connections in all parts of your memory, that even in the later stages of dementia, they were still fully there.

She wished those memories didn't exist. She tried to imagine this scene at Applebottom Park instead, the lake spread before them, and her gracefully aging mother sitting alongside them.

It was a pretty picture.

Luke still held the orange soda in his hand. "I'm mighty sorry. She sounds like a great lady."

"She was," Boone said. He looked off into the sky.

"Should I pour this into a couple of cups?" Luke asked.

Savannah sighed. "I guess so." She nudged Boone. "You ready to down this nasty stuff in honor of Mom?"

"If we have to." He grinned at her. They had this conversation every year. At least in the good years.

This was one of the good years.

"You know, I can see it's a tradition and all, but I could help you out," Luke said.

"How's that?" Savannah asked.

"Seems like the person who drinks your mom's soda shouldn't hate it."

"I'm all ears," Boone said.

"We thought about pouring it on her grave instead," Savannah said, "but we started feeling sorry for the grass."

Luke unscrewed the top. "I'll do it."

Savannah glanced at Boone. "Shall we let him?"

"He's volunteering? Definitely."

Luke tipped the bottle and downed it all in one long swig.

"Oh my gosh!" Savannah cried. "That was easy!"

"Of course it was," Luke said, replacing the cap. "I love orange soda." He lifted the bottle to the sky. "Thanks, Lena! I'm happy to take on your favorite."

Savannah's eyes pricked, and she scooted closer to Luke.

"That settles it then," Boone said. "Good thing you're already my son-in-law."

Savannah and Luke glanced at each other, and neither of them felt any need to correct him.

On the third day of spring break, it happened.

Savannah stood in the large yard, watching Luke and T-bone construct the portable outbuilding that would become the clinic come summer. Savannah had been keeping her eye on the dogs, who were a little out of sorts to be crowded in the small yard to keep them out of the men's way.

At first, it was just a bit of color barely visible from the corner of her eye.

It shouldn't be a butterfly, not at this time of year. Maybe it was a bit of trash blown over from the highway. It nagged at Savannah, so finally, she turned and gave the spot of color her full attention.

It was a bloom!

The bulbs Luke planted last fall were blooming!

She let out a little shriek, capturing Luke's attention.

"What is it?"

Savannah began running toward the gate. "The flowers! They're blooming!"

She raced around the fence toward her little garden.

Two bright yellow crocus and one pink tulip had almost fully opened. As she examined the flowers more carefully, she spotted three lilies and four anemones about to bud.

"You did it!" she cried out to Luke, who was approaching his side of the fence. "Look at them all!"

Luke leaned to peer down.

"Look at that," he said. "It worked."

"You don't fancy yourself a gardener then?"

"I've never grown flowers in my life."

T-bone joined them and gave Luke a hard nudge. "That means it's time, son."

Savannah glanced up. "Time for what?"

Luke coughed into his hand as T-bone elbowed him again. "Time to get some fertilizer. Gotta make sure they bloom good and strong."

T-bone let out a guffaw that sounded halfway like he was choking.

"Are you okay, T-bone?" Savannah asked.

Luke clapped his father on the shoulder, hard. "T-bone here has just got something stuck in his throat." Luke continued to hammer his back. "And it won't come out, will it?"

Savannah could tell something was up between the

two of them, but they were always acting like this. "Well, you two better get back to that construction. The clinic isn't going to build itself."

The men finished the building the next day, and T-bone declared that they should have a dedication ceremony.

Savannah suggested they wait until summer, when Luke would have his certification completed, and they could open the doors for real.

But T-bone would have nothing of it. The dedication would be that weekend, and he would have some of the townspeople come out and it would be a big ol' party with music and a barbecue.

Since she was overruled, on Friday afternoon, Savannah dug out one of her skirts, paired with tights and boots since it was still pretty chilly out. She didn't have a dressy coat, so she tracked down one of her mother's old scarves that had a bit of sparkle to it.

She Googled how to tie a scarf for half an hour before finally coming up with an arrangement that kept her neck warm and settled prettily over her shoulders.

It would have to do. No doubt the Tri-County News would be out to take a picture, and she wanted one of these few chances to be immortalized in the paper to have her looking decent.

As she settled the dogs in their kennels a bit early,

she heard hammering out back. She stepped outside to see several of T-bone's friends putting together a small stage.

She hurried out. "What's this?"

"It's just temporary," Fred assured her. "T-bone wanted to be able to see above the crowd."

The crowd?

Now that she was outside again, she spotted an entire line of barbecue smokers stretched along the fence. When had those arrived? And how many people were coming?

She got her answer within the hour. First, the helpers came. Men in aprons manned the smokers. Some of the ladies set up a table covered in pies. Savannah spotted Gertrude and Maude, and smiled when Maude gave her a little wink.

Miss Betty from the tea shop was there, setting up an entire five-tiered platter full of tiny teacakes, many of them sporting little dog heads made of frosting, something her decorator had gotten famous for.

Savannah admired them as more and more people arrived.

Tables were set up. The women quickly covered them with linen while others surrounded them with chairs. They were getting fancy, like this was a reception, not a dedication.

Then a man arrived with an audio system and large speakers.

"Do we really need all this?" she asked him as he unrolled a long extension cord.

He shrugged. "I just do what T-bone tells me."

The man himself finally came through the gate about an hour before the scheduled ceremony. Cars were filling up all of the space around her house, and two boys from the high school were out trying to keep order as the vehicles lined up in the fields.

Holy smokes, would all of them fit in her yard?

She texted Luke.

Did you know this was going to be so big?

His answer came quickly.

It got a little out of control. T-bone wanted a big party.

Savannah could see that!

Boone wandered out in the backyard to look at all the fuss. "What's going on here?" He seemed agitated.

Flo ran up behind him. "Sorry, he got away."

"We're having a little party, Boone," Savannah said quietly. "You want to stay out here for the barbecue?"

"You bet I do." He plopped down at one of the tables, and Flo settled next to him.

"I didn't know it was going to be so elaborate," Flo said. "I'm glad I came to help."

"I didn't know either."

Maude swiftly brought Boone a plate piled high with meat and sides, even though she shooed away anybody else who tried to get near the food. Soon he had a glass of tea and was kicked back, chowing on barbecue and grinning at everybody.

Savannah felt a hand circle her waist. She looked up at Luke. "You made it."

"Of course."

Something seemed off with him. He looked around, not meeting her eyes, jittery.

"You okay?"

"Right as rain. I'm going to check in with T-bone." He gave her a squeeze and headed over toward his father, who was directing the men at the barbecue grills.

Savannah sat down next to Flo and Boone. "This is really going to be something."

More and more people arrived, filling all the tables. Occasionally T-bone took the microphone and let everyone know that there would be food after a few announcements and the dedication.

As twilight began to descend, a set of pretty white lights flickered on, strung from the new building to the house. T-bone stepped back on the stage.

"I'm not a man of many words," he said. "But I want to thank you all for coming here as we celebrate the construction of the pet clinic at Lena's Home for Strays."

T-bone waved out toward the crowd. "Now I think Dr. Black, our local veterinarian, is going to say a few words."

Dr. Black emerged from the crowd. The two of them looked like pure opposites, T-bone in his leather vest and long beard, and Dr. Black in a tweed jacket and tie.

He took the mic from T-bone. "I'm very pleased to be sponsoring this tech clinic, a spot where many of the lost and homeless animals of Applebottom end up. We'll take the fine work started by Boone and Savannah in honor of Lena and expand it to include low-cost care for animals."

He searched the tables until his eyes met Savannah's. "I'm sure all of you would like to welcome up to the stage the people who made this happen, our very own Savannah Perkins and the man who will be our new vet tech, Luke Southard."

Oh. It was time. Savannah hopped up from her chair and meandered through the tables up to the stage.

She sure hoped she wasn't expected to speak. She'd assumed she would stand there and smile for a picture.

Luke also approached from the opposite side. He took her hand as she stepped up onto the platform.

Dr. Black passed the microphone to Luke and left the stage.

Luke continued to hold Savannah's hand, and Savannah felt a breath of relief. He was going to do the talking.

He lifted the mic. "It is so great to be here in front of you all. I don't think I've met everyone still, but I'm Luke, T-bone's son, and Savannah and I got this idea about five months ago to more or less formalize what we were already doing out here at the shelter. We fed newborn kittens. Nursed injured animals back to health. And with the extra procedures I'll be able to do with the license, we'll be able to provide even more services to animals in the area."

He drew Savannah closer to his side. "But that is only one of the reasons why you're here today. Truth be told, this clinic isn't going to open till summer, but we wanted an excuse to get you all here at the shelter tonight."

Savannah glanced over at him. What else was there?

"When I got here to Applebottom, I didn't have a stick of family," Luke said. "Then I met T-bone, and anybody who looks at us knows right off that clearly, this apple didn't fall far from the tree."

The crowd laughed and Savannah relaxed. Okay, so he was going to thank the community. Good.

"Now I have a lot of people in my corner, like Doc Black, and Doc Brigham, who's out there somewhere. And Fisher College. I nearly made the worst decision of my life to go back to Montana, but with the help of all of them, I got to stay."

The crowd cheered at this, and Luke paused and grinned. Savannah squeezed his hand.

"But now it's time to officially make myself a perma-nent part of the community." He drew in a shaky breath and Savannah turned to him, concerned. He was doing great. Why was he so nervous?

But then he dropped down on one knee, and it was her turn to zip straight through with shock.

"Savannah Leanora Perkins, you're not only the sunshine for all the animals in this county who get the love and attention of your care, but you are the brightest light for me, too. I want to help you continue your amazing work here, and I promise to do it with everything I've got."

Savannah could barely breathe. She forgot about the crowd, the new clinic, everything. All she could see was Luke.

"I know you will," she said.

"I'll try to be the man for the task, if you'll take me. Will you marry me?"

He let go of her hand and fumbled with his coat pocket for a moment, then managed to extricate a black velvet box. He opened it to reveal a lovely ring that she recognized as once belonging to her mother, albeit it with a little extra scrollwork on the sides now. Something old, something new.

She glanced out at Boone. He seemed absorbed in his pie, but at the quiet, he looked up and caught her expression. For a moment, his face seemed to clear, and he gave her a little nod before shoving his fork back into the crust.

She turned back to Luke. "I will," she said, tears squeezing out of her eyes. "Of course I will."

A great cheer went up as he slid the ring on her finger.

Music from the speakers began to play, and someone

shot off a couple of bottle rockets. Savannah laughed and shook her head at all the trouble T-bone had gone through for them. Luke was his only son, his surprise, and now she would be his daughter-in-law.

Luke stood up, his hand sliding up into her hair. His lips met hers, and another round of fireworks sizzled and broke open over the trees.

Her life might sometimes feel small, and her days filled with a lot of drudgery and sameness.

But today was special, and she was special. The sameness meant security for the animals in her care, something she would no longer have to do alone.

Savannah knew for certain now that the shelter she and her father had built would live on, just like her love for Luke.

Savannah and Luke will do so much good for Applebottom! They are stronger together.

Don't miss the wedding of Savannah and Luke, as witnessed by hard-talking, curmudgeonly Gertrude! Fans who receive text or email messages from Abby receive an exclusive bonus epilogue for every book!

Sign up on her web site for emails.

Or text ABBYT to 77948 (US only) for text!

Did you like Louisa and her gossip pizza? She will find *her* match and an instant family when Officer Stone unexpectedly gets custody of a newborn and has *no idea* what to do in the next Applebottom book *The Special Delivery*.

GERTRUDE & MAUDE'S LEMON CHESS PIE

(With blueberries, just for Savannah.)

CRUST

• **Any bottom-only pastry crust. Store bought is fine.**
(Maude, don't tell them to get store bought. That's like saying you should find your husband on the Internet.)
(But Gertie, lots of people DO find their husbands on the Internet.)
(Whatever for? There's old ladies everywhere to match them up!)
(I don't think so, Gertie. I think we're one of a kind.)
(But there's two of us.)

FILLING

- **4 eggs, separated into yolks and whites**

- **1/2 cup lemon juice**

- **3/4 cup sugar**

- **1/2 cup melted butter**

- **1 tablespoon flour**

- **1/2 cup fresh blueberries** (*If you have to use frozen, make sure they are thawed and remove any that are squished. Frozen blueberries will ruin the pie by slowing* *down the cooking around them. Squished ones won't make it through the top crust of the pie.)*

INSTRUCTIONS

1. Preheat the oven to 425°F.
2. For the crust: Lay a circle of crust on the bottom of the pie pan. Flute or fork the edges for decoration.
3. Cover with parchment paper and weight the paper down with dried beans or an oven-safe pot lid. (Gertie, did you know you could buy special weights for pie crust bottoms? *What would you buy those for? A pot lid works just fine!*

Gertie, you really should invest in nice things. *I'll invest in some hearing aids, so I can take them out when you talk about stuff I don't need!*)

4. Bake the pie crust for 4-5 minutes. Cool completely, 20-30 minutes. (Tell them what happens if they don't use the weight, Gertie. *It bubbles the crust.* And what about if the crust doesn't cool? *It'll be too wet and be all mushy. Happy now?* Yes, Gertie, I am. You're all boss and no information. *It's a recipe, Maude. It's supposed to be bossy.* What's it supposed to say? *If you don't mind, please gently put one lovely cup of sugar in the bowl?* I don't know, Gertie. The world might be mighty nice if everything gave instructions like that.)

1. Reheat the oven to 350°F.
2. Separate the eggs into white and yolks. (Have you tried the water-bottle method,

Gertie? I saw a YouTube video on how to do it. *Why would I watch YouTube to learn how to cook?* To learn new things! *Like using a water bottle to suck the yolk out of the whites?* So you did see it! *No. It was dumb.* But it worked, right? *Sure, if you're no good at doing it the normal way.* Oh, Gertie. You should be nicer.)

3. Beat the 4 egg whites on high speed with an electric mixer. They should form stiff peaks.

4. In another bowl, combine the 4 egg yolks, the sugar, and the melted butter. Whisk together until well blended.

5. Add the lemon juice to the egg yolk mixture.

6. Carefully fold in the egg whites. Do not overstir.

7. Pour the mixture into the piecrust bottom.

8. We recommend putting the pie on a cookie sheet, because you'll pull it out halfway through, and it will still be jelly-like.

9. Bake the pie at 350°F for 10 minutes.

10. Remove the pie and begin poking blueberries into the surface. A crust may have begun to form, so you will have to poke the blueberries in. You don't have to bury the blueberries. It's okay if they stick out.

11. Cook the pie for 20 more minutes. It should be firm and not jiggle. If it's jiggly, cook five more minutes. (What if it's still jiggly after

that, Gertie? *Then you blew it. Eat it with a spoon.)*

Enjoy your pie and don't miss more of Gertrude and Maude in the next Applebottom book: *The Special Delivery* !

Abby Tyler loves puppy dogs, pie, and small towns (she grew up in one!) Her Applebottom Matchmaker Society books combine the sweet and wholesome style of romance she loves with the funny, sometimes a-little-too-truthful characters she remembers from growing up in a place where everyone knew everybody's business.

Join her mail or text list for a bonus epilogue for every book, a wedding scene narrated by Gertrude!

The Applebottom Matchmaker Society books include:

- *The Sweetest Match*

- *The Perfect Disaster*
- *The Irresistible Spark*
- *The Unexpected Shelter*
- *The Special Delivery*

with many more planned!

facebook.com/authorabbytyler

twitter.com/abbytylerauthor

instagram.com/abbytylerauthor

bookbub.com/authors/abby-tyler

9 781938 150876